C.L. HOWLAND

THE GOOD LIFE

The Good Life

Copyright © 2019 by C. L. Howland

For information contact:

**http://www.clhowland.com**

Cover design by John Doppler

Publisher's Cataloging-in-Publication Data

Names: Howland, C. L., author.
Title: The good life / C.L. Howland.
Description: Santa Monica, CA : Random Tangent Press, 2019.
Identifiers: LCCN 2019906913 | ISBN 978-1-947957-07-7 (paperback) | ISBN 978-1-947957-08-4 (hardcover) | ISBN 978-1-947957-06-0 (ebook)
Subjects: LCSH: Single mothers--Fiction. | Sperm donors--Fiction. | Celebrities--Fiction. | Small cities--Fiction. | Man-woman relationships--Fiction. | Love--Fiction. | BISAC: FICTION / Women. | FICTION / Family Life / General. | FICTION / Small Town & Rural.
Classification: LCC PS3608.O95727 G66 2019 (print) | LCC PS3608.O95727 (ebook) | DDC 813.6--dc23.

First Edition: November 2019
RandomTangentPress.com
Santa Monica, CA

# Dedication

This book is dedicated to you, my readers, as thanks for your continued support. In this fun, light-hearted story, you'll meet new residents of Northam as well as visit with some of your favorite townspeople from previous books. Enjoy!

# Acknowledgements

As always, I'd like to thank God for my many blessings. This is The Good Life.

To my critique partners on this book, Carol J. Bova and Helen Lane—thanks, ladies, for all your insights.

Thanks to my beta readers for their feedback: CJ Alfonso and Jenna Ditcheos.

More than ever, I'd like to thank John Doppler from Random Tangent Press for his steadfast support in assisting me to bring stories to the world. You're an amazing man, John, and I'm lucky to have the opportunity to collaborate with you.

Also, a shout out to Clare at wiggoddess.com for my fabulous photos.

# Chapter 1

"I didn't think you'd ever waddle out here. Are you getting enough sleep?" Sherri Holt slipped through Madison O'Neill's door and past her pregnant friend without waiting for an answer. "You look like heck." The blonde breezed toward the back of the house. "You got any coffee?"

Madison stood in a daze, still holding the door knob. Swinging the door closed, she shook sleep-mussed hair. "No. I have tea though." She stifled a yawn before following Sherri to the kitchen.

"That herbal junk you drink? No thanks." Sherri dug through the large black bag she carried everywhere. "Here we go." Her grin was triumphant as she pulled out a small box and extracted a red foil packet. She filled a mug with tap water, shoved it in the microwave and punched several buttons. "Are you sick?" She narrowed her gaze. "You're usually up at the crack of dawn."

"I was. I'm dressed at least. I didn't sleep well and was just going to lie down for a few minutes. I must've dozed off." Maddie pushed back a few stray wisps of hair from her face. "I heard from the school board late yesterday afternoon."

"And?"

"Well, it's what I expected. My contract is up at the end of the school year. They're going to pay me until then, but they asked me not to return after Thanksgiving break."

"What? That's only a month away. It makes me so mad. Everything you've done for that school. They have no business dictating your personal life to begin with, and it's not your fault what that crazy doctor did. It certainly took them long enough to decide. You met with them a couple of months ago. Now, they're going to let you go—just before the baby is due? Idiots. What are you going to do?"

"Nothing right now. This whole thing with the doctor's gotten so much publicity; I just want it to die down." Madison sat at the table and pushed her hair back from her face. "Besides you, only the board members know I'm connected to this story, and I'd like to keep it that way."

"How long do you think that's going to last? Some of the biggest gossips in town are on the school board." Sherri jumped up at the ding of the microwave and fixed her coffee. She pulled a brush from her large handbag and began gently working it through Maddie's dark, thick hair, the same as when they were little girls and Sherri wanted to play dress up.

"I'm sure a couple of them would love to talk about it, but they've been warned it's an active investigation, so they're under a gag order."

"Any information yet about whether you received *stolen property*?"

"Very funny." Maddie poked her elbow in the general vicinity of her friend.

Sherri chuckled. "Sorry, I couldn't resist." She ran her fingers through Madison's now smooth hair before separating it and deftly beginning the intricate workings of a French braid. "Really, have you heard anything?"

"No, not yet. The Boston police said they were going to have to notify some of the donors, so they could sign waivers. After that, they'd tell everyone what was going on." Maddie sighed. "I don't have anything to worry about anyway. These special donors were celebrities, sports figures, intellectuals, people like that, and their *donations* were only offered to the wealthiest of clients. If Dr. Carson's daughter, Carleen, hadn't set it up, I wouldn't have even been able to afford his regular rates." Maddie paused for a moment, thinking of how Carleen hadn't returned any of her phone calls. "Can you imagine though? A network of nursing staff at hospitals all over the country stealing sperm to sell...it's incredible. I would've never thought such a thing of Dr. Carson."

Sherri gave a snort. "What's more incredible is—none of the guys remember it."

"According to Sergeant Dennison, they were only targeted if they were heavily sedated for something like surgery."

"Well, kiddo, knowing what you do now, would you still choose artificial insemination?" Sherri's bangle bracelets clinked in Maddie's ear as she continued to twist her hair into a braid.

Silent, Maddie pondered the question a moment. *Would I?* "Yes." She rubbed the side of her rounded abdomen.

"You should've taken Brian up on his offer, and you could've avoided this whole mess." Sherri wound a scrunchie around the end of Maddie's braid and let it drop.

"Sherri, you're not going to start this again, are you?"

"Well, my brother loves you and always has, ever since you ran Junior Sooner over."

Maddie grinned at her friend. She could still see the surprised look on Junior's pudgy face as he held a taller, but much lighter Brian Holt on the ground all those years ago. She'd only had her bigger bicycle for a couple of months and was still a little wobbly, but it didn't matter, she'd slammed into Junior full force. Despite her scraped knees and the bent front wheel, Madison managed to get back on her bike and keep going while Brian made his escape. It was the type of rescue repeated several more times over the years—at least until Maddie was thirteen and Junior caught up with her behind the town hall.

Instead of beating her up, he had other things in mind. By the time Brian got there, Junior was trying to get his hands under her shirt. Brian had pummeled the stockier boy in a way that went beyond a childhood scrap. Unable to watch, Maddie had crouched down by the wall of the building and heard Brian hiss, "Don't ever touch her again," before leading Madison away. Junior never had, or anyone else for that matter.

Sherri's older brother had grown to his full height of six foot four and weighed two fifty, with strong features and an easy smile that had every woman in town under eighty, and some over, loving him. *Why can't I?*

"You know I do Kathy Fuller's hair? Well, I just want you to know she's found an excuse to stop by the house to visit. Twice."

"That's nice." Maddie checked her hair in the mirror of the half bath off the kitchen. "Thanks for doing my hair. It's just what I needed. I feel much better."

Sherri slapped her hands against thighs encased in tight black jeans. "Don't you get it? She's trying to get him to ask her out!"

"That's good, right?" Maddie pulled on a baggy cardigan and scooped two net bags off the counter. "We want him to find someone, and Kathy's a nice girl."

"I guess so, if you like her type."

"And what type would that be?" Maddie raised a finely arched eyebrow.

"You know—still lives with mom and dad and goes out with a group of girls on Saturday night type." Sherri crossed her arms, rolling her eyes in exasperation. "It doesn't matter though. He didn't even blink in her direction."

"That's too bad. Look, I've got to get these bulbs in the ground before it gets too cold. Want to help?" Madison headed toward the back door.

"You're kidding, right? I just had these nails put on." Sherri followed, settling on the steps of the small farm porch. "I'll watch." She leaned back, resting her elbows on the porch floor, surrounded on both sides by several pots of chrysanthemums lining the steps.

"What a beautiful morning." Maddie inhaled, pulling cool air into her lungs. Dropping carefully to her knees, she rooted around with a trowel to loosen the dirt, enjoying the crispness of the fall morning. "I'm taking my students to the apple orchard two Saturdays from now—if we can finish raising the funds."

"Saturday? Why? That's not even a school day."

"I know, but it's when they can fit us in." Madison settled a bulb in the dirt, covered it and pointed her trowel at Sherri. "Don't forget we're having a bake sale at town hall this Saturday. And tell Brian I'm making his favorite chocolate chip cookies."

"Sounds exciting." Sherri's tone was less than enthusiastic as she shivered. "It's cold out here." She pulled the sleeves of her sweater over her hands and watched Maddie dig. "Brian could do that for you."

Sighing, Madison dug all the harder. "I don't need Brian to do this. I enjoy it."

"C'mon, Maddie. I can see my breath."

"Look, Sherri, I love you, but why are you here so early on a Sunday morning anyway?"

"God, I can't believe it. I almost forgot." Sherri leaned forward. "Willa Mae came in yesterday for her weekly hair appointment with Beulah. She'd just got done cleaning the Cohen place—someone finally rented it. Guess who it is?"

"Obviously, someone with money to burn."

"Come on, guess." When Maddie didn't answer right away, Sherri shook her hands, setting up the gypsy jingle of her bracelets again with her excitement.

"I don't know." Maddie shrugged. "Who?"

"Ring Stanford," Sherri said with a gush of excitement.

"The actor?"

"The actor? Duh! Of course the actor. He's so hot." Sherri looked deflated her friend didn't share her excitement. She continued on when Madison didn't respond. "You know that scandal sheet, *Hot Hollywood*? They're always running stories about him. He's not crazy or anything, I don't think—just kind of eccentric and wild—you know, drugs, parties, stuff like that. He's been in rehab, that I do know."

"Sherri, you don't believe everything you read in those tabloids, do you?" Madison wasn't able to hide the twitch of a bemused smile.

"Well, lots of it's true," Sherri insisted.

Madison kept digging.

"He also dated just about every actress in Hollywood before he got married." Sherri shook her head. "It doesn't make sense, what's he doing here?"

"I have no idea." *Ring Stanford.* Maddie had seen several of his movies. He'd played a variety of parts, some serious, some dark, but most with some kind of emotional baggage. Maddie liked his eyes. They were dark, almost as black as his hair. And haunting. The thought of his intense gaze sent an involuntary shiver through her. *Get a grip. It's acting; he's good at it.*

"Ring Stanford."

"Look, can we talk about something else?" Maddie muttered, working over a hard clump of frosty dirt with her trowel.

"No. He's here."

"What?" Glancing up at her friend's whispered words, Maddie was amazed to see Sherri sitting open-mouthed on the porch. Twisting around, she could hardly believe her own eyes. It really was Ring Stanford as if their conversation had conjured him. Maddie scrambled to her feet and brushed back a bit of stray hair, catching sight of her dirty hand out of the corner of her eye. Dumbstruck, it was several moments before she could ask, "Can I help you?"

"Are you Madison O'Neill?"

At her nod, the eyes she'd just been thinking of dropped to her mid-section. Self-conscious, Maddie fought the urge to cross her arms and instead pulled her sweater closed. "Can I help you?" she repeated, irritated at his rude stare.

"I'm Ring Stanford." His eyes were slow to return to her face. "I knocked at the front door, but no one answered. I heard voices out here, so I came around."

Those eyes locked on hers again. Maddie couldn't look away. His hair was long, but pulled back, accentuating prominent cheekbones. *Jingle, jingle, jingle.* Sherri tapped her on the shoulder. "I'm sorry. Mr. Stanford, this is my friend, Sherri Holt."

"How do you do?"

"I'm fine. Thanks," Sherri cooed.

Madison expected Sherri to melt into the path at any minute.

"Miss O'Neill, would it be possible to have a word with you?"

"Of course. What can I help you with?" *Maybe he has a child that needs tutoring?* Sherri did mention he was married. The extra money would help.

"I think we should talk in private." He glanced at Sherri again. "No offense."

"Well, I don't—"

"I understand, Mr. Stanford. Maybe we'll run into each other again." Sherri headed toward the back door. "I'll let myself out. Call me later," she tossed over her shoulder at Madison.

Noting the disappointment in her friend's voice, Maddie turned, but Sherri was already gone. She turned back in time to see Ring Stanford covertly staring at her stomach again. *Don't people still get pregnant in Hollywood?* "You needed to talk to me?"

"I'm not even sure where to begin." He ran a hand over his hair to the back of his neck and left it there, tipping his head back to flex muscles. "Maybe we should sit down?"

"Fine." She dropped down on the steps, waiting for him to sit. "No offense, but could you please tell me what this is all about?"

He paced back and forth on the walkway a minute before coming to a stop in front of her, examining one of several leather bracelets around his wrist. "I'm sure you know."

His words were abrupt. "Not a clue." She crossed her arms over raised knees.

He rubbed the back of his neck again. "Last year when I was in Boston to do a promo for a movie, someone shot me."

After a few moments of silence Maddie shifted under his intense scrutiny. "I remember reading something about it. Did they ever arrest anyone?"

"No. It was chalked up to the jealous spouse of a fan."

She couldn't miss the derision in his voice. "I'm sorry, Mr. Stanford, but I don't understand what this has to do with me."

"Of course not. Nothing comes to mind?" He stared at her. "Okay, I'll keep going. I ended up in an operating room having several bullets dug out. Afterward, while I was in recovery, someone removed something else. I didn't know about it until I got a call from a Sergeant Dennison of the Boston P.D."

"Mr. Stanford, you're going to have to stop talking in riddles. I don't see what any of this has to..." She stopped. *Sergeant Dennison? It can't be.* Without looking at him, Madison rose and moved away from the steps. "That's an interesting story, but as you can see, I'm really busy here." She moved back to the flower bed she'd abandoned earlier.

"Fine. How much do you want?"

"How much do I want for what? I have no idea what you're talking about." Tears welled. *This isn't happening.*

"Just tell me—what's your angle? Do you want one lump sum to split with the doctor? Or am I supposed to make payments?" His voice vibrated with anger.

*Is he crazy?* "Mr. Stanford, I don't want anything from you. I don't even know you."

"Give it up." He dropped to his knees, nose to nose with her, those eyes boring into her in accusation. "You know damn well I'm the baby's father."

"What? I didn't...you can't be...there has to be some mix up." Maddie shook her head. "The police told me the list was special. They said I needn't worry."

"There's no mix up."

"There has to be. You're Ring Stanford." Maddie swallowed the lump in her throat. "Why would he do that?"

"He's your friend, why don't you ask him?"

"It isn't like that. I hardly know him. My only connection is his daughter and I roomed together at college. She had some emotional issues, and I watched out for her, that's all." Hot, stinging tears formed behind her eyelids, but Maddie refused to succumb. She dropped her gaze and continued to shove bulbs into the dirt, heedless of her actions. *He thinks I did this on purpose?* Several tears mixed with the brown earth. She struggled to stand and moved to the steps without looking in his direction. "If it's true, thank you for taking the time to come and tell me. I'm sorry. I'm really tired. You'll have to excuse me." She hadn't climbed two steps when she heard his quiet reply.

"I haven't signed the waiver form."

She stopped. Turning, Madison was surprised to find him right behind her at the bottom of the steps. "Why?" Tears were leaking in earnest now, sliding down her cheeks. She didn't care.

"I wanted to see what your game was."

"Boy, you're thick." Madison shook her head. "This is not a game. I don't want your money, or anything to do with you. Just leave me alone."

"Not possible." He stared at her for a moment. "I've never really thought about kids, but thanks to you and the good doctor, I guess I have to now."

"I told you, I had nothing to do with this." Maddie used the sleeve of her sweater to wipe away the tears. "And there's nothing for you to think about—from what I understand you were out cold."

"You can act as indignant as you want, and out cold or not, that's my baby in there."

"It doesn't change anything. You need to sign the waiver. Please," she pleaded, deciding to change tactics. "I swear, I'll never tell a soul. The last thing I want is publicity."

"No more than I do, but it wouldn't be the first time my name made the papers."

*This has to be a dream.* Maddie closed her eyes and shook her head again as if that'd clear it. *No, he's still here.*

"I can't believe I'm saying this, but we need to be adult about this—"

"I assure you, Mr. Stanford, I'm an adult—"

"And figure out what to do about the situation." He continued speaking as if she hadn't interrupted. "So, let's get to the bottom line. What do you want from me?"

"Nothing."

"If I've learned anything, it's the fact everyone wants something."

Madison said nothing.

He studied her a moment. "Did you think I'd marry you or something?"

Maddie's jaw dropped as she shook her head. "I know you're married. Your wife must be furious."

"You need to catch up on your reading. My wife and I are separated and well on our way to a divorce." He put his hand up at the shocked look on Maddie's face. "Nothing to do with this. She doesn't even know about it. We've been apart for over a year."

"Sorry, I don't have time to keep abreast of all the goings-on in the celebrity world."

"Good to hear. There are so many worthier things to concentrate on." He gave her a wry smile. "Look, I've had my fill of wives right now, and maybe you don't want a husband, but we need to figure out—"

"Mr. Stanford, whether or not I want a husband is none of your business, and there's nothing to figure out. I'm going on with my life, and you are going to leave and go back to—to whatever it was you were doing."

"That I could...but I'm not leaving—I can't leave until we come to some sort of agreement."

*Agreement?* "Donors and recipients are supposed to remain anonymous. How'd you find me?"

He shrugged. "You'd be amazed at what money can buy." He rubbed the back of his neck and cleared his throat. "Look, I'm just going to come out and say this. Would you consider giving me the baby? It'll be well taken care of."

"Get off my property before I call the police," Maddie said with what composure she could muster.

"Miss O'Neill...as much as I'd like to, I'm not leaving this town until we come up with a workable solution for both of us."

"A workable solution? Sign the waiver. That works for me."

"I'm not signing the waiver." Those dark eyes pinned her in place.

"Stay away from me, or I'll call the police."

"I don't think so." And with that, he left Maddie standing there.

*He's right.* Maddie wouldn't call the police because then the whole world would know.

# Chapter 2

"Did you see her?"

"Yeah, I talked to her." Ring dropped onto the sofa, an exasperated sigh escaping his lips as he leaned his head back. *Breathe, Relax.*

"So? What's the deal?"

Everything was a deal to his manager of twelve years, Dave Martinez. "There's no deal."

"What do you mean? What does she want?"

"Nothing." The tightening in the pit of his stomach twisted another notch.

"Nothing?"

"That's what she said. I don't know if I believe it. I need a beer." Rising, Ring went to the fridge. "What's this? Where's my Utopia? Didn't you make the usual arrangements?"

Dave nodded. "Of course. The agency said the housekeeper would take care of it."

"Well, there must have been a miscommunication." Ring grabbed a beer from the lone four pack. "What's this stuff? Heady Topper?" He pulled the flip top and took a long drink. "Not bad."

He studied the can a moment before taking another swallow. "She says she wants me to sign the waiver form."

"That's it? No money? Boy, you do have a way with—"

"I'm not signing the paper, at least not yet."

"What? You're kidding, right? What are you, nuts?" Martinez exploded when Ring shook his head. "Look, I usually go along with whatever you want, but don't get mixed up in this. Just sign the damn paper so we can leave. Santos isn't going to hold off filming forever, you know."

"Maybe, but I'm not signing it." Ring walked to the sliding glass doors to stare out at the lake, watching the water sparkle in the midday sun.

"I told you to let me talk to her, to let me handle this," The swarthy man complained, sitting at the bar behind Ring. "But no, you had to come here to East Jockstrap and see for yourself."

Ring stood silent for several more moments. "Look at that foliage. It's incredible." He pointed to the mountains surrounding the lake, each splashed with shades of orange, red and yellow. "I'd forgotten how beautiful New England is in the fall."

"Yeah, it's a beaut," Dave answered, not even glancing that way. He paced to the refrigerator, glanced inside and shook his head before coming back to the bar. "You know Anne is going to put you through the wringer if—no when, she gets wind of this. Sooner or later, one of the bigger papers is going to pick up on the fact you're up here, and she'll send out the bloodhounds." He plopped on one of the stools. "Let me think a second." He stroked his mustache. "Okay, I'm sure with the right amount of money this woman will disappear."

"I told you, she claims she doesn't want money, and I don't think she's the type to just disappear," Ring said, coming to lean on the bar. "I think she has roots here."

"Yeah, what's your point? A tooth has roots too, but it can still be pulled."

Ring shook his head.

"Let me get this straight. You leave right in the middle of a movie to fly all this way, to meet a woman you didn't even knock up personally. Then she doesn't want anything from you but an autograph, and you don't want to give it to her? What exactly do you want, man?"

"I don't know." Ring studied the can a moment. "But she's not what I expected."

"What? You read the report. Thirty, single, school teacher. That about covers it."

"Yes, but she seemed surprised—"

"Surprised? Big deal. That just means she's a good actress. Wake up, Ring. You're the victim here. She's in cahoots with the doc. Anything is possible, especially if she needs to supplement whatever pittance she gets for a salary."

"$47, 475." Ring had read the file on Madison O'Neill so many times, he had it memorized.

"Really?" Dave whistled. "That little? Man, no wonder she went into the baby-making business. Seriously, what're you going to do?"

"I don't know. Maybe a kid is what I need." Ring hesitated. "Maybe I could raise it. Or something." He added at Dave's incredulous look.

"What are you, *loco*? What do you know about raising a kid?"

"Nothing, but I can hire someone."

Dave dug around under the bar and extracted a bottle. "I need a drink." He grabbed a highball glass, poured a healthy shot and downed it. "What is this stuff?" He glanced at the label and shivered. "Canadian whiskey? No wonder." He poured more and tossed it back again. This time, he didn't shiver. "Must I remind you; you're still technically married to one of the hottest actresses in the world?" Dave's voice echoed off the exposed beams far above their heads.

"She's the one who left me, remember? Has she signed the papers yet?"

"Nope. I just heard from the lawyers. Along with everything else, she now wants half of whatever revenue you earn from future projects."

"What?"

"Man, I tried to tell you not to marry her without a pre-nup, remember?"

Ring shrugged. "I was too high in those days to remember much of anything, but at this point, I'd give it to her if I believed it'd get her off my back."

"Are you shittin' me, Ring? This is incredible. You're killing your career; you know that? Rehab, the split up, then the shooting—now this. What's going on? Are you okay?"

"I'm fine."

Smoothing down his bushy black mustache, Dave thought for a moment. "Did she lay a guilt trip on you? That's it, isn't it? Look, how about if you sign the paper, and I'll go over and offer her some kind of monthly payment? That way everyone gets what they want. She gets your signature, and you get to help support the kid. That should work. We'll have to set the payment up through Stanco though, so no one will guess—"

"No. I understand your concern, but you handle my business affairs. This is personal."

"Don't kid yourself, Ring. Everything's business."

"Stay out of it, Dave." Ring walked toward the study. "I have some work to do." Powering up his laptop, Ring located the script he'd been reading.

"When was the last time you ate anything?" Dave stood in the doorway.

Ring shrugged.

"You've lost a lot of weight."

"I always do, you know that. I'll gain it back after the project's done."

"Maybe, but I haven't seen you this thin since you were—" Dave stopped.

"Since I was using?" Ring shook his head. "I'm not. When are you going to relax, Dave? It's been almost two years. I just have a lot on my mind."

"Yeah, I know, man, and I'm proud of you. I know it hasn't been easy, but I worry, especially when crap like this happens. Why don't I call out for lunch?"

"Call out? Look around, old boy. I don't think you'll find much for take-out around here. What'd you have in mind?"

"I don't know...maybe Thai?"

Ring shook his head. "I don't think so. You'd probably have to go back to where we landed yesterday."

"That far? Forget it. There's got to be someplace around here to get food. What'd that woman say?"

Ring didn't look up. "What woman?"

"The one who gave us the keys. The one who was supposed to have the place set up." Dave circled the top of his head with his hand a couple of times. "Remember, she looked like she had a ratty bird's nest sitting on her head?"

Ring nodded.

"She said something about a grocery store, somewhere around here. Vance's, Vince's, something like that. Maybe we should hire a chef while we're here. What do you think?"

"Huh?" Ring looked up from the computer screen. "Think about what?"

"Hiring someone to do meals?"

Ring sighed. "I don't care, Dave, whatever you figure out will be fine, though I doubt you'll find much around here."

"Great. I can see the headlines now. Big star and manager starve to death in the wilds of Vermont. No way. I'm finding someone tomorrow. Right now, I'm having the driver take me to the nearest restaurant."

After Dave left, Ring watched the cursor on the screen, idling at an accusatory blink as he replayed the scene with Madison O'Neill over in his mind. He'd carried the waiver since arriving in Boston, after the police had notified him. He could've stayed in Mexico and had the forms sent to him. Instead, he'd talked the director into giving him a few weeks off, much to Dave's horror. When the police wouldn't divulge who the recipient was, it hadn't taken the private investigator he'd hired long to find out who it was and where she lived.

Madison O'Neill was different than anyone in his world, not to mention she was carrying his child. As far as he knew that was a claim no one else had ever been able to make. *Don't get too excited, she's very likely in cahoots with the doctor.* Still, she interested him, and he hadn't been interested in much of anything in a long time. Until he figured out her game and what to do about the child, he wasn't going anywhere.

Ring went to bed, only to toss and turn. *I need to get back to my own life—and if necessary, bring this baby with me.* Though the thought was alien, it brought a slight smile to Ring's lips as he drifted off. *A baby.*

# Chapter 3

"Okay, everyone, remember, good circle behavior," Maddie reminded the shifting six-year-olds on the carpet at her feet, patient while they formed a rough semi-circle again. "We have a few minutes before it's time to go. Would anyone like to share what they're wearing for a costume tonight?" Several tiny hands popped up. "Darcy?"

"A fairy princess."

Maddie smiled at the little girl. "Anyone else?" She glanced toward the door as she listened, catching a glimpse of a face in the window. *Ring Stanford? What's he doing here?* She jumped up and worked her way around several squirming bodies. "Keep talking, Jeffrey," she prompted, swinging open the door to check the hallway. Empty. Maddie shook her head and closed the door as the dismissal bell rang. She produced a weak smile for her students. "Let's get our coats and line up, shall we?" Assembled in a crooked line at the door, Maddie reminded her students of the safety tips they'd gone over earlier in the day for trick-or-treating before being barraged with a loud chorus of goodbyes as the children exited the room.

Uneasy, Madison gathered her book bag. *Maybe I imagined him.* Ring Stanford had been in Northam for almost two weeks. It seemed he was everywhere. No one except Sherri knew he'd come to visit her, and despite her friend's insistent teasing, Maddie wouldn't tell her what he wanted. A celebrity in a town the size of Northam caused quite a stir, and she couldn't seem to go anywhere without hearing something about Ring Stanford.

"Night, Maddie."

"Goodnight, Winona." Winona Evans was the new teacher in the room next door.

"I hear Ring Stanford might be having dinner down at the China Breeze tonight. Tom and I were going there for dinner anyway since it's coupon night. You want to go?"

"No thanks." Maddie closed her classroom door. "But thanks for the offer." That was the last thing she needed, a confrontation with Ring Stanford in the tiny take-out joint, while at least half the town watched the encounter over their discount egg rolls and Scorpion Bowls.

Ten minutes later, she pulled into her driveway.

"Hi, Maddie."

She flipped the front seat forward and turned toward the familiar voice. "Hi, Brian," she called before hauling her book bag out of the car.

Brian pulled off work gloves and ambled toward her. "Do you need help?"

"No. It's fine. What're you doing here?"

"I told you I'd stop by and work on the wall." Brian indicated a now uniform section of the stone wall along the edge of the drive.

"That looks great. Thanks, but you didn't have to do it right away. Sherri told me how busy you are."

Square, clean cut features formed a smile. "Business has been good this year."

Madison could hear the note of pride in his voice.

"I've got some things in the works, and if everything goes as planned, I think I'll be able to keep most of the guys working all· winter."

"That's great." Seasonal occupations like construction made it tough on several local families in the winter. Brian's family had been one. A gust of wind rustled the bundles of corn stalks decorating the front porch and had Maddie shivering under her coat. "Want some coffee?" she asked, noticing his red cheeks. "Sherri brought a box of those instant packets she likes so much and left them here."

"Sure. Just let me put my tools away. It's about quitting time anyway—one of the perks of being the boss." His grin was sheepish.

Half an hour later, after Brian laid a fire in the living room fireplace, they sat at the kitchen table. "Thanks for starting the fire. It'll be nice later. Would you like to sit in there?"

Brian shook his head. "No, this is fine. I don't want to mess it up with my work clothes. Can I let you in on a secret?"

"Of course."

"Business has been good lately. Real good. And if everything works out, it's only going to get better. I've been thinking, I should be able to build Sherri her own shop in the spring."

"What? Oh, Brian, that's great. She's always wanted her own place. She's going to love it." Maddie's thoughts drifted as Brian continued on about his plans. *He could be a poster child for the all-American boy with that smile.* Maddie leaned on her fist, listening to him talk. *How could two such plain people as Esther and Burton Holt have ever produced such a specimen? I wonder who the baby will look like, me or—never mind.* She focused on Brian's words again.

A few minutes later, a knock at the front door interrupted Brian. Glancing out the window, Maddie realized it was dark outside. "I bet it's some trick or treaters. Would you answer the door while I get some goodies out?" As she ripped open a bag of wrapped fruit snacks, she could hear Brian's deep voice. "Here we go," she called, coming around the corner with a large aluminum bowl and an even larger smile. "Happy Halloween." The words died on her lips. It was Ring Stanford.

"Hi. I hope I'm not interrupting anything." Ring glanced from Maddie to Brian and then back to Maddie again.

"This is Brian Holt." She chose to ignore his pointed remark. "Brian, this is Ring Stanford."

Brian was doing some sizing up of his own. Maddie could tell Sherri had told at least one person about her visitor by the look on his face. His stance was tense with arms folded across his chest, and one she'd come to recognize over the years. *This will never do.*

Neither man acknowledged the other for several moments. She elbowed Brian, and he reluctantly stuck out his hand. The handshake was brief. Maddie didn't even reach the top of Brian's shoulder, but she could see a muscle in his jaw working. *This is too much.* "Was there something you wanted?" she asked Ring, hoping her voice didn't betray her nervousness.

"The same thing I've been trying to talk to you about for two weeks." He seemed oblivious to the evil looks Brian directed his way at the cryptic answer.

*I'm just putting off the inevitable. Maybe if I talk to him, he'll go away.* According to the lawyer she'd talked to in Burlington earlier in the week, he had a lot of rights to this baby, even as far as suing for custody. "Half an hour. That's it."

The slam of a car door caught Maddie's attention. Two witches and a vampire headed up the street followed by a heavyset woman. *Great. The way her hair's teased, it can only be Willa Mae Carter. That's all I need, to have one of the biggest busybodies in town see Ring Stanford on my porch.* Maddie hauled him inside and slammed the door before shoving the bowl of treats into Brian's hand. She stepped to the side of the door, out of sight, taking Ring with her. A loud knock sounded, and Brian gave her a *what's going on?* look.

"It's Willa Mae," Maddie whispered. "Just give her kids some treats."

Shrugging broad shoulders, Brian swung open the door.

"Trick or treat."

"Here you go."

Maddie could hear the rustle of plastic as Brian dropped packages into each bag. Sandwiched behind the door with Ring, she could feel his breath at her temple and smell the warm, clean scent of his aftershave.

"Hey, Brian. Who was in that big black car that just took off?"

"I have no idea what you're talking about."

"You're handing out candy for Maddie?"

"That I am, Willa Mae. Are you kids going to the party at the fire station?"

"Yup. We came out early so we can get some extra candy for Daddy's lunch."

"Hush up now, Marvie." By the sound, Willa'd thumped the chubby boy on the back. "Is something happening I don't know about? Is that girl going to finally marry you or what?"

*Boy, no one can grill 'em like Willa Mae.*

"Not yet, but I'm working on it." Brian answered, his tone good-natured.

"You kids go on back to the car. I'll be right along."

*What's she up to?*

"Tell me the truth, Brian. That baby's yours, ain't it?" Willa Mae whispered. "You can tell me. I won't tell no one."

*No, you'll tell everyone.*

"Willa, you've got a dirty mind," was all Brian said.

*Thanks, Brian. That ought to be some new fodder for the gossip mill.* Maddie glanced up and found Ring studying her face as he too listened to the conversation on the other side of the door.

"Bye, Willa. See you later. Tell Marv I said hi." Brian closed the protective portal.

"Brian Holt. How dare you?" Maddie's voice was a whispered hiss. "To Willa Mae, of all people."

"What? I only told the truth," he answered, all innocence. "I haven't given up."

Maddie shook her head. "I'm talking about the baby."

"Maddie, you know Willa's gonna say what she wants no matter what you tell her. Besides, I've told you before..." he stopped and glanced at Ring before clearing his throat. "I'd treat this baby like my own, you know that. It doesn't matter how you got it."

His earnest words brought an immediate scowl to Ring Stanford's face.

*I'd better break this up before any revelations are made.* Maddie stepped forward and slipped an arm around Brian's waist. "We've been all through this, Bri." Her voice was soft as she led him toward the back of the house. "It's getting late, and Sherri will have your supper made by now." Pulling his coat off the back of the kitchen chair, she handed it to him.

Brian hesitated a moment before slipping it on. "Are you going to be okay?"

The phone rang. "I'll be fine. Honest." Madison reached for the receiver. "Hello?" Listening for a moment, she nodded. "Yes, I have. He's still here. Hold on a minute. I'll pass it on. It's Sherri. She says to get a move on; she's trying a new recipe in the crock pot." Madison smiled at Brian's grimace. "And the meat's starting to disintegrate." Brian shook his head. "He's leaving right now."

"Fine. But I'll check with you later." Brian headed out the back door.

Madison hung up the receiver and moved to the stove to turn on the teakettle. "You have half an hour," she reminded Ring, without turning around.

"Is he your boyfriend?"

"That's none of your business." *Men. Why don't they just beat on their chests and get it over with?* "Mr. Stanford, is that what you wanted to talk about?" She turned to lean against the counter.

"I want to talk about anyone who has an interest in my child."

Maddie sighed. "Remember Sherri, the girl you met here? Brian's her brother. I've known him my entire life, and he's a good friend."

"He wants to be more than friends."

*I can't believe I'm having this conversation.* "Look, Brian's my friend. End of discussion." She was rarely short with people, but she'd been on edge ever since Ring Stanford had shown up in town. *You need to calm down or you'll be crying again.* "I'm sorry. It's been a long day, and I'm really tired. I haven't been sleeping well." Maddie massaged her temple.

He studied her for a moment before nodding. "Me neither." He hesitated again. "I've been doing a lot of thinking."

"Me too." Maddie cleared her throat. "Look, Mr. Stanford, please believe me when I say I knew nothing about Dr. Carson's scheme." She braced herself for more of his accusations. Instead, he said nothing, just continued to watch her. *He's listening, at least. Maybe I can reason with him.* She shifted under his steady gaze. "I'm sorry you got caught up in this. Please know I'm very capable of raising this baby." *Maybe I can get him to sign the release form now.* She indicated a chair. "Would you like to sit down?"

He nodded. "In a minute. Do you like Chinese food?"

The question wasn't what she expected. "Yes, but I don't—"

"I'll be right back."

# Chapter 4

*What's he doing?* Maddie sat at the table with her tea. *Chinese food? I can't be seen with him.* She heard the door open. "I can't go—" She stopped.

Ring stood in the opening to the kitchen with a tall man in a dark suit. "This is—what's your name again?"

"Harold, sir." The man held several large brown paper bags.

"Right, Harold. You can lay out the table. How about in the dining room?" Ring stepped back into the living room and pointed. "It's right there."

The man nodded and headed that way to survey the room a moment before turning to Madison. "Ma'am, I assume your linens are in the sideboard?"

"Linens? That won't be necessary. I haven't laid a fire in the dining room in ages." She smiled at the man. "Harold, the kitchen is warmer. Just put the food on the counter. I'll set the table. Will you be eating with us?"

The man covered his surprise with a smile as he set the food down. "Ahh, thank you, ma'am, but no." He stepped back and directed his attention to Ring. "Will there be anything else, sir?"

Ring shook his head. "It seems not."

"Very good. Whenever you're ready, sir. Ma'am." The man touched black gloved fingers to the brim of the black hat he wore before turning to leave.

Maddie waited for the front door to close. "Was that a chauffeur?"

Ring nodded.

"He's English. You have an English chauffeur?"

"Yes, I suppose so, at the moment at least. He's not my regular driver, just one hired to drive me while I'm here."

"What? You don't drive yourself?"

"Not usually."

"And you picked up food from the China Breeze?"

Ring shrugged. "No, the chauffeur picked it up."

*That getup must have set the place on its ear!* "Is he driving a limo?"

"What else would he be driving?"

"Where'd he go?" She didn't wait for an answer but hurried to open the front door. Sure enough, a black limousine sat on the other side of the stonewall at the edge of the road. An old pickup truck approached and slowed to a crawl as its headlights hit the shiny finish of the car. Maddie slammed the door. "You have to make him leave. He can't park there."

"Why?"

"Because everyone will know you're here. I can't have that. Please, you have to get him to leave."

"And go where?"

"I don't know. I don't know." She paced a moment. "There's a garage on the next road over, have him park there. There are always lots of cars in the parking lot."

"Do you think that's necessary?"

Madison marched to the front door and opened it. "Yes. Either he moves now, or you'll have to take your food and go with him." She waited.

"Fine." He was back in a few minutes. "He's gone."

"Good. Thank you."

"You're welcome. Shall we eat?"

Maddie eyed the bags. "What'd you do, order one of everything?"

He shrugged. "You're hungry, aren't you? You have to eat. I'm starved today, it must be the air here. I thought we could talk and eat at the same time."

"Well, I am hungry," Maddie admitted. Her unease dissipated a bit. "I had playground duty today and didn't have much of a chance for lunch. Do you want to get the food out while I get plates?"

"Oh. Sure." He shrugged off his coat and blew on tanned hands. "It's getting really chilly out there."

"Actually, it's usually colder than this. I remember once when I was a little girl I had to wear my snowsuit and boots under my costume..." Madison trailed off, the memory filling her with unexpected warmth. She sighed and looked up to find him studying her from the other side of the table. *Be careful here.* Madison jumped up. "Would you like something to drink? Tea? Or instant coffee? I also have milk or orange juice." She opened the refrigerator. "I don't have much in the way of spirits, but Sherri left some kind of wine coolers here, if you're interested."

"Tea? I haven't had tea in a long time. Tea would be great." He placed white cartons on the table. "You grew up here?"

"Born and raised." She took another mug out of the cupboard, filled it with hot water from the kettle and dropped a tea bag in to steep. "Here you go." She placed the cup on the table. "There's honey on the counter if you want it."

"Does your family still live here?"

Reaching up in the cupboard, she paused before pulling down plates. "They did. Both of my parents and my older brother, Josh, were killed eight years ago in an automobile accident." Maddie kept her back to him as she gathered silverware from a drawer.

"I'm sorry."

"Me too." She gave him a sad smile as she arranged the utensils on the table.

"Do you have other family?"

"One aunt in Massachusetts. She was married to my father's brother. My mother was an only child." Maddie tucked napkins under the forks as she glanced at the table and then did a double take. Take out cartons covered the table top. "Wow, this is crazy. This is so much food."

"Hopefully you'll find something you like then."

She shook her head. "I'm sure I will."

He indicated the table. "Shall we?"

She'd just slid into a chair when headlights flashed across the kitchen window. *The limo driver again?* Maddie pulled the curtain aside. *More trick or treaters.* "Excuse me. I'll be right back." She hurried toward the front of the house to scoop up the bowl from the side table and open the door before anyone could knock. "Happy Halloween."

"Trick or treat, Ms. O'Neill."

Maddie bent to take a closer look as she dropped brightly wrapped packages into the outstretched plastic bucket. "My, my. A fairy princess. How beautiful you look. The other fairies must be jealous," she gushed as the little girl giggled. Pushing the mask atop her head, Darcy Simms grinned, showing the gap of missing front teeth. "It's me."

Maddie laid a hand alongside her cheek in mock surprise. "I would've never known. Where's baby Simon?"

"He fell asleep while we were at the fire station, so we're goin' home, but Mommy said I could stop here."

"Wonderful. Well, take some for him too. Bye, see you in school tomorrow." She stepped out onto the porch and waved at the waiting car before closing the door, only to find Ring on the other side.

"One of my students." *How long has he been standing there?* "The food must be getting cold." She moved past him.

He followed her back to the kitchen. "You like kids, don't you?"

She nodded. "I do."

They settled at the table again.

"Ms. O'Neill, we need to talk about the baby."

*Here it comes. Relax. You have to work through this. It's going to be all right.* "Please call me Madison, or Maddie."

"Okay. If you call me Ring."

They filled their plates in silence.

"So, Madison, what are your plans?"

"As far as what? The baby?" She set her fork down. "Mr. Stanford—Ring," she corrected at his scowl, "I told you earlier. I can take care of this baby."

"Who's going to take care of it while you work?"

"Well, at the moment, that's a non-issue. I'll be done at school when we start Thanksgiving break."

"What then?"

She shrugged. "Nothing for a few months, at least until after the baby is born. My parents' life insurance paid off the mortgage, and I've saved enough to take about six months off before I have to start looking for work again." She took a sip of her tea. "And I can always tutor."

"You're not going back to the school?"

Maddie shook her head. They ate in silence for several minutes.

"When are you supposed to have the baby?"

"If everything goes right around the beginning of January."

"Why wouldn't everything go right?"

Maddie looked up, surprised at the concern she saw etched on his features. "It will. It's just I've been told by lots of women that babies come when they want, not when the doctor says." *Why am I reassuring him?* She wasn't sure. To cover her discomfort, Maddie picked up her plate and carried it to the sink. *Relax. Stay calm.* "Do you mind if I ask you a personal question?"

"It's why I'm here."

"I know you said you and your wife are separated." She hesitated for a moment. "And Sherri told me you had no children although you were married for a while. Why? I mean you're obviously interested," she queried, trying not to sound defensive.

Ring stood and set his plate on the counter. "There were complications." He leaned a hip against the counter and crossed his arms.

Madison flushed. "I'm sorry. I hadn't thought of a medical problem."

"It wasn't medical. When Anne and I—"

"You don't have to explain. It's none of my business."

"It is. The baby you're carrying gives you the right. My wife and I partied hard—for years. I stopped, she didn't want to." He shrugged. "I don't think either of us ever gave a thought to having kids. One thing led to another—she became interested in someone else, so we parted ways."

"I'm sorry."

"Don't be," Ring shook his head. "It was definitely for the best. What's your story?"

"I beg your pardon?"

"Your friend, Brian, looks as healthy as a redwood, and more than willing to do the marriage, babies, mortgage thing. Why'd you opt for the unknown?"

"Brian's a good person. I've known him forever; and I do love him, just not like that. He's more like a brother to me. It wouldn't be fair to either of us."

"What about adoption?"

"I thought of adoption, but to be honest, I wanted O'Neill blood to be part of this baby. I know it sounds selfish, but I can't help it." She paused. "It was important too—for the rest of my family. They were good people. My brother was only twenty-six years old when the accident happened. He never got a chance to be a husband or a father. And my parents never got the chance to spoil grandchildren. They should have." Maddie glanced away as tears welled in her eyes. *Darn hormones.*

"It doesn't sound selfish. It makes perfect sense to me."

"It does?"

He nodded. "I don't have much to offer as far as family, but the baby does have a grandmother."

"Really?"

"Don't sound so surprised." His tone was dry. "I do have a mother. She lives in New Jersey."

"New Jersey? How'd you end up on the West Coast?"

"My parents were both from Jersey originally. They joined a church. One that, I guess, would be considered a cult nowadays. My father was ordained, and right after I was born, they went to Central America as missionaries. A few years later, the church broke up, and we moved on, getting as far as California before the money ran out. Then my father decided he wanted to be an actor, and my mother went to work in a diner." Ring gave a dry chuckle. "My mother had a better run as a waitress. He was never around much, but this one time, when I was nine, he decided to drag me along on one of his auditions. The director asked me to audition for another movie he was working on. I said no. My father said yes, so I did. I got the role, and my father got a role too—as my agent. His best performance ever, some might say, and I guess the rest is history."

*There's no joy in his voice. What's the whole story?*

"Anyway, my father died when I was seventeen, and my Mother wanted to move back to New Jersey."

"Would you like more tea?" Maddie asked, not sure why she felt the need to lighten the mood.

"Sure. My mom and I used to drink tea all the time."

She put the kettle on and returned for their mugs. Maddie gasped and laid her hand on the side of her abdomen for a moment before rubbing it a few times.

"What's wrong?"

"Nothing really. The baby gave me a hard kick."

His shoulders visibly relaxed. "Really?" Curiosity etched his features.

*He looks like one of my students.* Unable to resist, the teacher in Maddie took over as she held out a hand. "Would you like to feel?"

Ring's hand rose hesitantly. "Where?"

With a small smile, she placed it alongside the silky material of her top. For a few moments they waited, but nothing happened. "Maybe he won't do it—" she stopped as the baby kicked again, making her gasp before laughing. "He's a strong one."

Fine lines creased the corners of warm dark eyes as Ring openly smiled for the first time. *He should do that more often.* She stared at him, mesmerized by his smile. He hadn't moved his hand and the width of his long fingers splayed over the thin material felt warm and strangely comforting. Feeling awkward as he continued to hold his hand there, Maddie cleared her throat.

He dropped his hand. "You said he. It's a boy?"

"I don't know for sure. *He* just fits for some reason." Maddie sat down again. "Look, you needn't worry. I'll be a good mother. I have enough tutoring lined up for next year, so there isn't an issue of being able to support the baby."

Ring sat down and leaned forward. "I want..." he trailed off and rubbed the back of his neck in what was fast becoming a familiar gesture to Maddie. *Does he do it when he's stressed?* "You want what?"

He dropped his hand to his lap. "I want..." He stopped. His hand was at the back of his neck again. Maddie waited, but nothing could have prepared her for his next words.

"I want the chance to be a father."

# Chapter 5

Maddie sat upright in her chair. "What?"

The surprise on her features echoed the surprise Ring felt as he uttered the statement. *But it's true. I do.* The thought had been at the back of his mind for several days, Ring just hadn't brought it forth to examine it. His nod was slight at first but turned vehement. "I do. I want to be a father."

"You don't know what you're talking about." Maddie shook her head in denial just as vigorously as he was nodding. "You have no clue."

"Yes, I do."

"No, you don't. This isn't a role in some movie. You don't come and go as you please. Children need continuity, not someone who roams in and out of their life every year or two."

"Do you think I don't know that? I know that. Believe me. I'd never do that...my father did it to me for years."

"All the more reason not to get involved—"

"Yes, it is. I'll never be my father." His tone was harsh. "Never. I don't want my baby to grow up without a father."

"We don't even know each other."

He scooted his chair closer, his long legs resting against the outside of her knees. "Then we need to get to know each other, for the baby's sake." His gaze locked onto hers, holding her in place. "Please. Get to know me before you make a judgment. That's all I'm asking." He paused. "Please."

"How can I do that? This is a small town. If we're seen together, everyone will know, and I won't get a moment's peace."

*This will never work unless I can get her away from here.* "We could go somewhere else for a few weeks."

Madison raised her eyebrows, but remained silent.

"All above board. I'll even have a chaperone, if you want."

"I don't think so. That's all I need is for someone to see us. I've already lost my job, thanks to the Dr. Carson scandal. I don't need this on top of it."

"What do you mean? I saw you there today."

"So, you were at the door. That's a relief. I thought I was hallucinating. Wait." Her eyes narrowed with suspicion. "Why were you there?"

"I was waiting to talk to you. But some old lady came along, and said I'd have to sign in at the office, so I left. You didn't get fired because I showed up there, did you?"

"No. They don't even know about you. I can't imagine what they'd do if they did." Madison sighed. "It seems Northam wasn't as progressive as I had always assumed, or the school board at least. They called me to a meeting when it became apparent I was pregnant, and asked if I intended to marry the father. For some reason, I think they found that more acceptable than when I told them it was artificial insemination. Anyway, *The Great Sperm Caper,* as Sherri likes to call it, was the icing on the cake."

"Look, you said you're done at Thanksgiving—what if I find a place I guarantee is private, will you come for the holiday?"

"I can't just pick up and leave. I have things going on. I need to pack up my classroom, and I'm on the Harvest Ball committee."

"Harvest Ball? A ball? Here? As in gowns and tux?"

"Ball is a lofty title, but that's probably because it's been going on for close to a hundred and fifty years. It's really more like a town dance, but everyone comes." Maddie shook her head and smiled. "But alas no, no tux. Though I guess you could wear one. There are a few suits, some string ties and dress shirts. The standard is usually a new flannel shirt and a pair of Sunday Carhartts. But the women now, that's a different story. Everyone "dolls up". Long dresses, short dresses, you name it. And for weeks after, it'll be the topic of conversation wherever you go. My dad used to laugh and ask what my mother and I were wearing to the *Peacock Parade*. My mom was the home economics teacher at the high school, so she made us new dresses every year."

"Can you skip it this once?"

Maddie shook her head. "No. And I don't want to. I've helped with it ever since I can remember."

"Okay. How about this? I'm filming in Mexico. If I find a private house, would you consider coming after the Harvest thing? For Thanksgiving?"

Maddie shook her head again. "I always have Thanksgiving with Brian and Sherri."

*She isn't making this easy.* Ring rubbed his neck again. "Fine. Bring them too."

"That'll be really expensive. I don't think I can afford—"

"Don't worry about the cost. I'll take care of it."

"That doesn't feel right. Most people around here don't get something if they can't afford to pay for it. Sherri and Brian are no different."

"Okay. Well, I can always buy that shack I'm staying in right now and camp out indefinitely once filming is over."

"The Cohen house is one of the nicest places on the lake."

Ring snorted. "Have you ever been in there?"

Maddie shook her head.

"Then how do you know it's nice?"

"People have said so."

"Okay, so what's it to be?"

"What do you mean?"

"Are you and your friends coming on vacation, or am I going to have to buy the Taj Mahal of Northam, Vermont?"

"I'm not too worried about it. If I remember the gossip correctly, Cy Cohen paid almost three million for that place over ten years ago."

"And what's your point, besides he got ripped off?"

"You couldn't afford it."

He said nothing.

"Could you?"

"There's one way to find out."

Neither of them said anything for a few moments.

She sighed. "Fine, I'll ask. But I don't think Brian is going to be too keen on going."

"That's a shame."

"Yeah, sure it is." She gave him a slight smile. "I thought you're supposed to be a big-time actor. That wasn't very convincing."

"Well, some people think I am, if the Golden Globes on my mother's mantle and Academy nominations are any indication. So, just you and Sherri then?"

"I'm sure Sherri would love to go, but with Christmas coming I don't know if—"

"Good. Think of it as an opportunity for Sherri," he cut Madison off. "I'll take care of everything. No one will even know we're together; I promise. You can come and go as you please...shop, eat, lay on the beach, whatever you want."

"That does sound tempting. I'll talk to Sherri, but I'm not promising anything."

*Convince her.* He laid a hand over hers. "Thank you for considering it."

Madison blushed and rose quickly, only to sway and grasp the edge of the table.

"Are you all right?"

"Yes, I just stood up too fast. I guess I'm more tired than I thought. I'd better clean this up and go to bed." She closed a carton on the table.

"Why don't you put your feet up?"

"And who's going to take care of all this food?"

"Leave it."

"Are you crazy? There's a fortune in food here." But Ring was already guiding her toward the living room. "It'll just take a minute to—"

"I'll toss it."

"What? You can't throw it away."

"What am I supposed to do with it?"

"I don't know, but you can't throw it away. Take some with you."

"I suppose I could take some to Dave. He still hasn't found a cook."

"Who's Dave?"

"My manager. He came here with me. We don't cook, so he's been doing a lot of riding around to find takeout."

She nodded. "I need to put a little more wood on the fire."

"I'll do it. Have a seat."

She sank down on the sofa.

"Would you like another cup of tea? I can manage that much— I think."

Before Madison could answer a knock sounded on the front door. They stared at each other in uncertainty for a moment. Maddie pushed to the edge of the sofa and then stood. Ring was there to steady her.

"Are you still dizzy?"

Maddie closed her eyes for a moment. "Maybe a little."

"I'll tell them to go away."

"No, you can't do that!"

"Why not?"

"No."

"Fine. Don't answer the door then."

Maddie exhaled. "No, I have to. I'm okay." She gave him a weak smile. "Why don't you pack the food up? Take some and put the rest in the fridge. I'll take it to school tomorrow for the teachers." She walked to the door and turned, her hand resting on the knob. "I'm okay."

Unconvinced, Ring nonetheless headed to the kitchen. He finally got her tea together and returned to the living room. She was settled on the sofa.

"Here's your tea."

"Thanks." She took a sip and leaned her head back.

"Isn't it getting late for trick-or-treaters?"

She shrugged. "The party at the fire station just got over, so they're making last minute rounds. I can't blame them. I remember lugging in a big bag of Halloween candy like a trophy and my mother letting me pick three pieces before she put it away. Of course, nobody ever mentioned how much candy I'd already eaten."

"All that sugar couldn't have been good for you."

"Don't tell me you didn't sneak candy out of your bag?"

He shook his head.

"You're kidding?"

"I never went trick or treating."

"What?"

"My father didn't believe in it."

"Which part?"

Ring cleared his throat. "All of it. The costumes, the candy, the parties. He used to say it was all part of satanism. The devil's youth group."

"No offense, but that's ridiculous."

"My mother tried to tell him that too. Just once."

A frown marred Madison's features. "What about other holidays?"

Ring shook his head. *How do I explain life with my father? Easy, I don't.* He glanced around the room. "Your house is small, but it's cozy."

"Small? You wouldn't think so if you had to pay the heating bills. But thank you, I guess. It was built by the Wellman family— you know, Wellman Tools?"

"Everyone knows Wellman Tools. I didn't realize it was here."

She nodded. "It's not, anymore. The factory closed in the early '50's. The whole thing is kind of sad. My grandparents bought the house after most of the family was killed at Pearl Harbor." Maddie glanced around the room. "It's a pretty typical New England Federal—large and drafty. The antiques are worn, the hardwood floors scuffed and my grandmother's oriental rugs are pretty threadbare, but it's home and I love every tired inch of it." A sad smile curved her lips. "My dad called it the money pit, but my mom called it our haven. She used to say no matter what else was going on in our lives, it was our safe space. And she was right. It was. Always." Her last words were barely above a whisper as she studied the crackling fire.

"You were lucky to have such a place."

Madison stirred at the briefest touch on her cheek. It took several minutes for her to come fully awake. She pushed down the afghan she hadn't remembered covering up with, yawned and scrubbed her hands over her face. *Maybe I was dreaming.* The last thing she remembered was the warmth from the fireplace and being tired. A piece of paper, the size of a business card, leaned against a chunky candle on the coffee table. She reached for it. The handwriting was a mixture of printing and cursive in the small space. Maddie was surprised to see misspellings.

*Madison, thank you for talking to me and for shareing not only a meal, but a bit of yoreself. I'll be in touch very soon. Get some rest. My number is on the other side if you need me. —Ring PS I dont spel very well. Sorry.*

She turned the card over. It was a business card with his name and several numbers printed on it. There was also a handwritten number scrawled across the bottom. Maddie turned it back over and read the message again, shaking her head. *Nope, I'm definitely not dreaming. If I were, he'd be a better speller.*

# Chapter 6

Brian wouldn't be thrilled about the invitation, so Maddie proposed she and Sherri take a mini vacation and left it at that. She felt bad about not telling Brian everything, but she hadn't told Sherri the whole story yet either. That didn't stop her friend from purchasing a new wardrobe. In between preparations for the Harvest Ball and packing up her classroom, Madison stitched up a couple of light dresses. She finally relented and ordered a maternity bathing suit on-line. Hopefully, it would be here soon. They were leaving the day after Thanksgiving. *I can't believe it's less than a week away.*

Ring Stanford was no longer in Northam. He'd left right after they'd had dinner, but had called Madison almost every day over the last couple of weeks. Each time they talked, she'd ask how the movie was going and fill him in on the latest catastrophe in planning the Ball, and they'd end up laughing about it. She'd even talked to his manager, Dave Martinez, just this afternoon. He let her know all the arrangements were made, and Ring would contact her soon. Maddie thanked him and hung up.

If only her disappointment at not talking to Ring was as easy to cast off as the robe she'd just tossed on the bed. Maddie shook her head. "Get over it." She carefully pulled her dress on over her head, trying not to mess up her hair. She smoothed the soft material down over her body and managed to close the last few buttons she'd left open at the back to get her head through and went to work on the row of buttons on each sleeve.

Once Sherri saw her dress for tonight, she'd pestered Maddie about fixing her hair. Not one to visit the salon, especially the day of the Harvest Ball, she struck a deal with Sherri. If she'd come by the house and do it after work, Maddie would bake her some coconut macaroons.

Sherri had left most of Maddie's hair down long, pulling back the top and side sections and working them into an intricate basket weave of braids as she intertwined pale green and emerald green satin ribbons. Maddie had to admit it was the perfect hairstyle for the green velvet dress as she studied her reflection in the mirror, using a hand mirror to check the back of her head. *Good job, M'Lady. It's still intact.* She turned from one side to the other. The off the shoulder neckline and snug sleeves looked okay and the empire waist of the gown flowed away from her torso, semi-disguising her advancing pregnancy. *Who are you trying to kid? You're almost seven months pregnant, there's not much that can disguise that.* She added some light touches of makeup and lifted the hem of her dress to slip her feet into pale green satin flats before glancing in the long mirror one more time. *Mom would've liked this one.*

The high school parking lot was almost full when she pulled in. *Wow, we're going to have a good turnout this year.* An hour later, it was evident her prediction was accurate. People were elbow to elbow, if not on the dance floor, then in groups amongst the pumpkins, cornstalks and hay bale seating placed throughout the gym.

Maddie danced with Albie Norstock and promised Brian a waltz later. She smiled as he danced by with Willa Mae Carter. Somehow, Willa's beehive hairdo looked even bigger tonight. That, in combination with high heels and a very tight A-line dress reminded Maddie of a well-fed Marge Simpson.

Willa Mae let out a whoop and almost took Brian off his feet as she swung him around. "Woo hoo, Brian Holt. You're one heck of a dancer. Okay, let's go then." He gave Maddie an imploring look before the older woman whirled him away, deeper into the crowd.

Maddie laughed and shook her head. *He might be too tired by the time we get around to that waltz.*

"Did you see that? I didn't realize Willa Mae was that strong."

Maddie turned to grin at Sherri while shaking her head. "Poor Brian."

"He'll survive." Sherri took a sip of her drink. "I've been looking for you."

"What's up? Marv isn't dispensing his hard cider, is he?"

Sherri shrugged. "I have no clue. I did see him and some other guys over in the corner, but I didn't pay that much attention."

Maddie made a mental note to check on the group. Every year, while Willa danced with anyone who couldn't get away, her husband sat on the sidelines imbibing the homemade brew with his cronies.

"Anyway, I wanted to tell you..." Sherri leaned in and lowered her voice. "Guess who I saw come in a few minutes ago?"

"I have no idea. Most of the town is already here."

"Ring Stanford."

"What? You're kidding? Where?"

"Last I saw him, he was talking to one of the selectmen and Mr. Whitman over on the other side of the gym."

Without thinking, Maddie headed that way. She stopped as Ring led Virginia Whitman out onto the floor.

"Hi, Maddie."

*Missy Stone. No, it was Missy Freeman now. Missy Easton? Or was she back to Missy Stone?*

"Nice dress. Did ya make it? No, don't bother answerin'. I know you did. You always have the best dresses for this thing."

"Thank you." Maddie kept her eyes on the dance floor.

"Can you believe Ring Stanford is back? I wonder what he's doing here?" Missy snapped her gum. "You gonna try and get him to sign something?"

*How could she possibly know?* Maddie cut her eyes over to the other woman. "What?"

"Are you going to have him sign something? An autograph?"

Relief washed over Maddie. "No."

"Me, I'm goin' to get a dance. I told Mr. W. I'd really like to meet him and get an autograph. For Blair."

"Where is Blair?"

Missy stepped closer. "Rehab. Again. She smashed right into that nightclub in West Lebanon. They tried to keep it quiet, but she had to see a judge this time. One more time and she goes to jail."

"That's too bad." Blair Whitman was always in trouble, ever since they were kids. The sad thing was, she brought most of it on herself.

"Look at that, they called switch partners. He's dancing with Mina Mouse now."

Maddie glanced at the dance floor. Ring was indeed dancing with Mina Mason Miller, her smile shy as she glanced up at the tall man. "Don't call her that."

"Sorry. I don't mean nothin' by it. It's just what Blair called her when we were in school."

"We're not in school anymore."

Missy shrugged. "True, but she made out okay. She married Sam Miller. Lucky girl. I wouldn't kick his shoes out from under my bed. What?" She questioned at Maddie's sharp look. "It's true. I wouldn't, and evidently Mina wouldn't either. How many kids do they have now? Three? And another one on the way. Holy cow! That's a lot of kids."

Maddie made no comment and turned her gaze back to the dance floor. Ring led the small woman around the floor in a slow circle to the waltz, leaving her husband, Samuel Two Bears Miller, to partner Virginia Whitman. Sam looked none too happy about it, holding the older woman in a stiff embrace.

Missy gave a snorting laugh. "Ha. Sam and Mrs. W.? That's funny. They can't stand each other." She sighed. "Yeah, but look at Sam. He can't take his eyes off Mina, even with her as pregnant as she is." The plump woman sighed again. "Lucky girl."

Maddie decided to ignore the pregnancy comment. Missy was one of those people who seemed to have no filter when it came to speaking. Whatever thought ran through her brain made a direct exit out of her mouth, but in this case, she was right. Sam's attention was on his wife, and Maddie was willing to bet he couldn't wait for this dance to be over.

"Hey, maybe you're in luck. You're at least as pregnant as Mina. Maybe Ring Stanford likes pregnant women."

*Okay, that's way too close to home.* "Look, Missy—" She never got to finish. The music ended, followed by a smattering of applause.

"Here he comes." Missy located the top edge of her pantyhose right through her outfit and gave them a yank, before tugging down the hem of her short dress. She fluffed up her frost-tipped, spiked hair and rubbed her lips back and forth against each other a couple of times. "How do I look? Any lipstick on my teeth?" She turned to Maddie, the move setting her large hoop earrings in motion as she pulled her lips back, exposing teeth abused for years by coffee and cigarettes.

"No, you're good."

"Great." Missy gave another tug on her dress. "You got a breath mint?"

Maddie shook her head.

"Crap. Oh well...Mrs. W., how are ya?" Missy stepped toward the group coming off the dance floor.

"Hello, Melissa. How are you?"

Madison hung back as Virginia introduced Missy to Ring Stanford.

"Hi, Maddie. How are you?" Mina came to stand by her side, followed by Sam.

"I'm good. How about yourself?"

"I'm fine. Just about ready for this to be over." Mina rubbed the top of her extended abdomen.

Mina's hand was covered by the large brown hand of her husband as Sam Miller slid his arms around her and pulled her close to nuzzle her neck. "You look beautiful. Hi, Madison, how are you doing?" He gave her a warm smile, exposing white teeth.

Maddie's throat tightened, and she unconsciously rested her hand on her own distended torso. It was obvious these two were in love. She cleared her throat. "I'm fine, Sam. How are things with you?"

"Couldn't be better." His grin was even wider, if that was possible. "Did Brian tell you the news?"

"News? What news?"

"I'll let him tell you. Hey, Brian." Sam extended his hand while keeping an arm wrapped around his wife.

Brian Holt shook the proffered hand. "Hi, Sam. Mina." The tall man directed his attention to Maddie and shook his head. "Thanks for saving me from Willa."

Maddie shrugged. "Sorry."

"Yeah, I can tell by that smile just how sorry you are."

She made a face at him. He made one back, and they both laughed—kids again for a moment. He dropped an arm around her shoulders and gave a light squeeze.

"Sam says you have some news. What's up?"

"Remember I told you work was going well?"

She nodded.

"And you know Sam went into business for himself too?"

Maddie nodded again.

"Well, instead of being in competition, we decided it would be better for both companies and our employees if we went into partnership. Because of that, we have work lined up clear through next winter," Brian finished with a smile.

Maddie patted Brian's shirt front with the flat of her hand in her excitement, resting it there as she smiled up at him. "Bri, that's great."

He gave her shoulders another squeeze. "I think so too."

"Excuse me, everyone. May I interrupt a moment to introduce Mr. Stanford?"

Maddie's head pivoted toward Virginia Whitman. Ring was at her side. His gaze rested on her a moment before giving his attention to what Virginia was saying. *What was that look about? He looked...hurt? About what?*

"Mr. Stanford—sorry, I forgot. Ring." Virginia turned an apologetic grin on Ring. "Ring is thinking of purchasing real estate, perhaps in Northam." She gave him another smile, "and wanted to know a little more about the town. So, Matt and I said we'd introduce him around. You've met Mina. This is her husband, Sam Miller." Ring extended his hand and Sam shook it with a nod.

"This is Brian Holt. Both he and Sam are local builders."

Brian spoke before Ring had time to extend his hand. "We've met."

"Oh..." Virginia cleared her throat. "Well, good. Okay. Ah, this is Madison O'Neill. She is—was a teacher at the elementary school. We have an excellent school system."

Neither of them moved for a moment. Was he waiting for her cue? Madison extended her hand. "It's nice to meet you, Mr. Stanford." She'd forgotten Brian still had his arm around her until she felt his grip tighten at her words.

"Please call me Ring. It's nice to meet you too, Madison." He took her hand in both of his. His fingers were warm as they grazed her wrist, the light touch generating a shiver up the inside of her arm. Startled at the sensation, she looked up into the eyes that had begun to haunt her hours, awake and asleep.

"You have a nice town here."

"Ah, yes. Thank you." Somehow, through no more than the minimal touch of a handshake, he'd managed to draw her forward, or had she moved on her own volition? Maddie was aware of music and movement around them. Still they stood, their eyes as firmly clasped as their hands.

"Dance?"

She wasn't sure if he'd said the word out loud or merely mouthed it, but at her slight nod, he slid an arm around her and left the group behind.

"Hey, Mrs. W., I thought it was supposed to be my turn for a dance?"

*Missy?*

His dark eyes held hers captive even as they moved amongst the other dancers. "How are you?" His words were low and soft, almost a caress.

"I'm fine. How are you?"

"Better now that I'm here." He wore a dark suit, but had removed his tie, and his shirt was unbuttoned at the collar. "Just tired."

"What are you doing here?" Maddie blushed. "I'm sorry. That's none of my business."

"Don't be sorry. There were predictions of a tropical storm and rather than risk it, production was shut down for the weekend. It'll put us behind, but no one complained...the last couple of weeks, we've been working twenty hours a day. I had business to attend to, but I'd heard so much about the preparation for this ball, I had to come and see how it turned out." His smile was tinged with fatigue, but there was a faint glint of humor in his eyes.

"You go to the Academy Awards—and you wanted to see this? Hay bales and homemade ice cream?"

He nodded, his eyes leaving her face a moment as he surveyed the cavernous room. "You described it well. I like it. The awards shows...every event that happens there is a competition, with or without awards. Even the parties—actors compete with other actors to talk to directors. Directors compete with other directors to get to the big dollar producers and so on up the food chain. There's lots of posing and posturing while everybody takes a shot at everyone else in the room."

"That doesn't even sound like fun."

He shook his head. "It's not. If Dave didn't constantly harp on me, I wouldn't go to any of it."

"I never thought of it like that. All you ever see on television are beautiful women in gorgeous gowns."

"None of them have anything on you. You look beautiful tonight."

She blushed again, in both embarrassment and pleasure. "That's kind of you to say, but I'm well aware of how I look right now...this was about the only style I could make to accommodate—" she stopped.

"Our baby?"

His words were quiet, but Maddie glanced around anyway. They were surrounded by other dancers, and for the first time, she noticed the stares. *Oh, great, everyone's watching me moon over him.* She nodded. "Are you really looking at real estate in Northam?" she asked, hoping to change the subject.

He shrugged. "Who knows?"

As they worked their way around the room, Maddie caught sight of Missy past his left shoulder, alternating between waving her arms wildly and tugging on her dress. "Ahh, I think there are other ladies waiting to dance with you."

He followed her line of sight and sighed. "Okay, I admit the real estate thing may have been a bit of a ruse...it was the only way I could think of to talk to you, but I'm not sure how much more *meet and greet* I can take."

Missy hopped up and down.

"You wouldn't consider rescuing me, would you?"

Maddie shook her head. "I can't. For lots of these women, a dance with you will probably be the most exciting thing that ever happens to them. I'm not going to be responsible for taking that away. You got yourself into this."

Ring sighed. "Okay, teacher, I get it. I'll finish what I started, but do you think maybe we can get together later, after this?"

"I don't know. It's going to be late by the time we get done cleaning up tonight."

"I'll stay and help."

Maddie shook her head. *No way—Willa will be all over that.* "That's not necessary. Our committee does setup and take down. It's all very organized."

"You're not actually taking anything down, right? You're supervising?"

She shrugged. "I do what I can."

"All this extra work has to be hard on you. Why don't you take it easy? You might hurt yourself. How about I send the driver in to help?"

She laughed and shook her head. "No, thank you. I'm fine. I'm not going to hurt myself. Or the baby." Her last words were delivered in a quiet voice as they approached Missy. He didn't look convinced. "I'm fine."

"Hey, Ring, I think it's my turn." Missy stepped out onto the dance floor in an effective block, leaving them no choice but to stop. "Maddie, you must be gettin' tired, carrying around all that extra weight." She gave Maddie a big smile.

"I'd say she weighs less—"

"I am getting a little tired," Maddie cut Ring off. "Thanks for taking over, Missy." *She has no clue.* The other woman's next words confirmed Maddie's thought.

"No problem. I'm always willing to help out a friend." She turned in Ring's direction. "It's just the kind of girl I am. Oh, Maddie, I almost forgot, I was supposed to give you some messages when you came off the dance floor. Let me see, Mrs. Johnson says they're almost out of cider and wants to know if you have any more. Also, Chief Lawson is looking for you—he said there are cars parked in the fire lane that need to be moved and..." she hesitated. "Who else? Oh, yeah, how could I forget? Mrs. Edgars is looking for you—something about running out of ballots. Again." Missy stepped closer to Ring. "For king and queen. Gee, I'd love to win this year. I spent big bucks on this dress. You like it?"

"It's very...colorful."

"Thanks. Ya ready?" Missy beamed and held up her arms. "What's the matter?"

"Nothing. I'm sorry." Ring stepped forward, and Missy latched on, snugging herself up against him and draping her arms over his shoulders. He gently, but firmly slid her arms down and arranged them in the traditional waltz pose. "It's easier to talk this way."

"Talk? Ah, yeah, sure..." She agreed when he turned that famous gaze on her.

"Miss O'Neill, thank you for the dance. I look forward to conversing with you again. Soon."

Maddie nodded.

"Conversin'? Now there's a swanky word." Missy laughed, already moving, not waiting for Ring to lead. "Yeah, I think I have a pretty good chance of gettin' queen this year since my friend, Blair, isn't here—she always wins."

They moved away, and Maddie left the dance floor. She headed toward the ice cream table in search of Mabel Edgars when a loud laugh caught her attention. *Oh, no you don't.* Maddie put on her sternest teacher face and switched directions.

# Chapter 7

Marv Carter and several other men sat in a group of closely placed chairs. Marv slapped the seat of the metal chair next to him as he spoke to Fred Edgars. Fred plopped down on the chair, his long legs sprawled out in front of him as Marv thumped him on the back a couple of times.

"Hello, Marv....gentlemen. How are you all this evening?"

"Pretty good, Maddie. How 'bout yourself?" Marv relaxed in his chair, his hand and cup resting on his protruding belly.

"I'm fine, thank you. Are you having a good time?"

Marv shrugged. "Yeah, as long as Willa ain't pesterin' me." The group laughed.

"How 'bout you, Maddie? You been havin' a good time?"

*Junior Sooner.* He may have never touched her again after Brian's warning when they were kids, but any interaction with him gave Maddie a queasy feeling. His grinning leer and pointed stare at her stomach served to accentuate his question. She ignored him. "Marv, what's in the cup?"

"The same as usual. Look what Willa found me." He reached down beside his chair with a grunt. "These coffee pot things. They hold a lot more than a thermos." He held up a silver air pot by the handle and balanced it on his wide thigh. "You just put your cup under the spout, like this, and give it a pump." The demonstration filled his cup to the brim.

"Maybe Maddie would like a pump or two."

Madison's face colored.

Marv turned to the younger man. "Shut up, Junior. Dammit, now look what you made me do. I spilled my drink." He sat the pot down and tugged a bandanna from his pocket, mopping at his lap. "I look like I can't hold my water." The other men snickered.

Maddie shook her head. *Somebody else can deal with these guys for once. I just need to get Fred away from them.* She turned to the lanky man. "Hi Fred, how are you?"

Fred Edgars lived on the outskirts of town on the family farm. He was a little slow and never finished school, but he had a good heart, always willing to help anyone who asked. Tonight his hair was slicked back. Maddie wasn't sure if it was wet or he had something in it, but either way it accentuated the large black plastic frame glasses he always wore.

"I'm greeaat," he answered in his best Tony-the-Tiger imitation and grinned. One of his top teeth, just off center, was missing.

"Fred, what happened to your tooth?"

"A calf kicked me."

Maddie grimaced. "I'm sorry. That had to hurt."

"Yup." He scrubbed his fingers along the side of his nose and then scratched his ruddy cheek. "At first."

"Fred, have you been drinking Marv's cider?"

Fred sat upright in the chair. "No, ma'am. My ma would kill me."

The music changed, a popular country song that generated foot stomping and lots of whoops, even from this small group.

"Maddie, you wanna dance?"

"Fred, why would she want to dance with a manure-smellin' retard like you?"

"Shut up, Junior." Fred's wide grin was gone, his ruddy cheeks even redder as he slumped forward. "I ain't no retard, I'm smart. Ain't I, Maddie?"

"You certainly are." Madison wasn't sure she had the energy to keep up with Fred's dance style, but it was worth a try if it got him away from this group. "And I'd love to dance with you."

Fred's grin was back as he pivoted toward Junior. "She'd love to dance with me, so there, butt-head." He sprang to his feet.

"And Marv, I'm going to let Chief Lawson know about your fondness for hard cider since he's new."

"So what? What's the cowboy cop from Texas gonna do? We ain't driving." The man's chubby features shifted into a lazy grin.

"See that you don't." Madison turned away. "Ready, Fred?"

"Ready Freddie, that's me!" He jerked a thumb at his chest.

"Well, okay then." She took a breath and held out a hand. "Here we go."

Fred hauled her out on the floor, swinging her into his renowned version of a polka/two-step dance combo. She caught Brian's concerned expression out of the corner of her eye. He stepped forward, and Maddie gave a slight head shake as she flew by with Fred.

*Okay, this isn't too bad.* She flashed Fred a slight smile as he hooted and grinned at her. For the most part, Maddie concentrated on trying to follow his crazy steps. She kept up with him for most of the song, despite her breath coming in short pants. *The last chorus. It's almost over, hang on, just a few more seconds.* Fred gave another whoop and twirled Maddie. It caught her by surprise, and she had no time to adjust, the added bulk of her belly throwing her off balance. She stumbled and fell, landing hard on her knees and sliding several feet, thanks to the velvet material of her dress and highly polished gym floor, only stopping when she hit a pair of legs in high heels.

"Maddie!"

*The baby. The baby.* She bent forward to protect her abdomen. She'd heard Fred's frightened shout, but couldn't catch her breath. Several small pieces of papers slid to a stop at her knees. *Ballots?* She glanced at them as she attempted to suck air in through her mouth. *They're all filled out?* Someone lifted her off the floor. *I'm okay. Put me down.* She didn't have enough breath to get the words out. *Who'd I run into?*

She glanced back to see Missy Stone scrambling around on the floor, her dress hiked to the top of her thighs. She didn't seem to notice; she was busy stuffing slips of paper into her purse.

"Hang on, Madison."

The words were whispered into her ear. *Ring? He's carrying me?*

"I'm okay," she huffed as she fought for air. "Please put me down."

"Take her to my office."

*Coach Markett?* She was lowered onto a vinyl-cushioned table.

"Madison? Are you okay? Where does it hurt?"

She brought her head up to look into Ring's worried eyes.

Maddie managed to whisper, "I'm okay."

"Are you sure? Are you in pain?"

She dropped her eyes again as she continued to suck in much needed oxygen. He rested a hand on each of her thighs, but she doubted he was aware of it. Maddie caught movement out of the corner of her eye and shifted her gaze. The room was crowded with people and there were more in the hallway. She sucked in two large breaths. "I'm fine. I just got the wind knocked out of me." She raised her head and gave the group a weak smile as she used the palms of her hands to slide Ring's hands off her legs in a nonchalant movement. "I'm okay, really. Is Missy okay?"

"She's fine."

Maddie shifted her gaze. *Willa Mae.* The woman stood behind Ring, watching with interest. *Great.*

"Okay, folks. Why don't you all go back and enjoy yourselves and give Madison some air?" The basketball coach, Jim Markett spoke up. "Let's go. Nurse Betty will be here in a minute." He ushered people toward the doorway. "I'd feel better if you'd at least let Betty check you out."

Maddie nodded. Betty Edgars worked at the nursing home and was Fred's aunt. *Fred?* "Where's Fred?"

"Who?" Ring hadn't moved.

"The man I was dancing with?"

Ring shook his head. "I have no idea, but I'd like to talk to him too."

Maddie glanced around the room. Everyone was out of earshot. "It's not Fred's fault. He's just...exuberant."

"Exuberant or drunk?"

"He doesn't drink." Only Brian and Sherri stood outside in the hall now. "Sherri, would you find Fred for me? I need to talk to him." Sherri nodded and left. "Bri, would you help her?"

"You gonna be okay?"

She smiled at her longtime friend, touched, as always, by his concern. "Yes, I'm fine. Really—go." She shooed him when he made no move to leave.

"I'll be right back."

Maddie waited until Brian turned the corner before speaking. "You need to leave too."

"What?"

"I'm sure people are already wondering why you picked me up, and why you're still in here since we were just introduced tonight."

"I want to make sure you and the baby are okay."

"You can't stay."

"I don't care what people say."

"That's because you don't live here. I do. Please."

He stared at her for several moments.

"Please." Footsteps echoed at the end of the tiled hallway.

"Fine." He nodded. "But I'm coming by later and checking on you."

"I didn't mean to." Maddie heard Fred Edgar's voice as the footsteps came closer. "I didn't mean to."

"It's okay, Fred. She just wants to talk to you." Sherri's voice.

"Fine, but you have to leave now." Maddie pasted a smile on her face as Fred came through the door. "Hi, Fred."

"Hi, Maddie. I'm real sorry."

Fred had his arms crossed and Maddie could see his eyes were red behind his thick glasses.

"I didn't mean to hurt you." He swallowed hard, making his Adam's apple bob as a tear slid down his mottled red cheek.

"Fred, you didn't hurt me."

"You're okay?"

She nodded and tapped the seat next to her.

Fred came to lean against the table. "I'm sorry for knockin' you down, Maddie."

She put an arm around him and gave him a pat on the back. "You didn't knock me down, I tripped, that's all. I'm a little clumsy these days."

"That's okay, I'm clumsy sometimes too." He gave her a tremulous smile.

Betty Edgars came through the door. "Okay, everyone...let's give Madison some privacy."

"Why's Aunt Betty here, if you're okay?"

"Just to check me out. Honest. I've got to be ready for the next time we dance, don't I?"

Fred nodded.

Betty walked to the door. "Freddie, why don't you see if you can help out with cleanup, and we'll send Madison home early tonight."

"Sure, Aunt Betty. Maddie, I'll see you soon."

With a wave of her arm as imperious as any general, Nurse Betty finished clearing the room.

# Chapter 8

"Thanks, you guys. I really appreciate it."

"Are you sure you're okay? Do you want me to stay overnight?"

Maddie shook her head and then rested her cheek against the edge of the door as she smiled at her friends. "No, Sherri, you go on home and get some sleep. That's what I'm going to do. I'm fine, really. Thanks again for being my chauffeur. How are you going to get your car now?"

"I'll take her back tomorrow afternoon," Brian volunteered. "We can bring yours back too."

"That'd be great. Thanks again."

They turned to leave.

"Goodnight."

"Night. I'll call you tomorrow," Sherri tossed over her shoulder.

"Okay." Maddie closed the door and leaned against it. *You've got to move while you can.* She pushed away from the door and worked her way through the living room, using the sofa to steady herself. *Laundry room for a nightgown first. Then the bathroom.*

*Only a few more steps.* Half an hour later, Maddie sank to the sofa in front of the fireplace, placing a bag of ice wrapped in a towel gently on her knees. "Ahh," she sighed in relief.

Nurse Betty had checked her vision, pulse and blood pressure and asked her questions pertaining to the pregnancy. Satisfied, she said Maddie could go home, but if she had any spotting or cramps she was, as Nurse Betty put it, to high-tail it to the hospital. Maddie wanted to get home, so she agreed and didn't mention her knees, managing to keep her gait as normal as possible the few steps to the car and then to the house. Even when she finally got her dress off and slipped into the soft worn flannel nightgown, she didn't take time to look. She just needed to sit down.

*Hmm, the fire feels good.* Maddie swung her stiff legs up on the couch as she leaned back to rest against the throw pillows. *I could fall asleep right here.* She tugged the afghan off the back of the couch and pulled it over herself. *I think I will. I'm not sure I can make it upstairs.*

Maddie sat up, startled awake. *What was that?* She listened, but heard nothing. *It must have been my imagination. What time is it?* She checked the mantle clock, she'd only been asleep half an hour. She was about to lay back down when she heard the noise again. A light tap. *A knock? Is someone knocking at the door?* She glanced over the back of the sofa toward the front door. *There it is again. The back door, someone's at the back door.*

Maddie swung her feet to the floor and slid forward, her knees aching in protest at the motion. They felt worse than before she sat down. Four steps and she was at the opening of the kitchen, six more and she was at the counter. *Okay, just a couple of more. You can do this.* The knock sounded again. *C'mon. Move.* She put her hand on the door frame to steady herself and pulled the door open. Ring stood there.

"Hi. I was beginning to wonder when you didn't answer. Are you okay?"

She nodded and continued to clutch the door frame.

"May I come in?"

She nodded again and let go of the door, so it swung open.

"I know how you are about it, so I had the driver drop me off on the next street over and walked here." He closed the door behind him. "You weren't in bed, were you?"

"No. Not yet. Why don't you make yourself comfortable in the living room, maybe add a log to the fire? I'll be right in."

He headed off, and she leaned back against the wall. *You can do this.* And she did until she reached the doorway to the living room. *It's only a few more steps.* She just couldn't make her knees bend to take another step.

"That's all set." Ring brushed his hands off and turned to her. "What's wrong? Is it the baby?"

She shook her head, her balance now precarious on unstable legs. "My knees. Could you help me to the couch?"

He came at her, and she held up a hand. "Please don't pick me up again. An arm to lean on is really all I need." He slid an arm around her back, and she leaned on him as she took small steps to the sofa. "Now I know how my grandma felt at eighty-five," she joked as Ring helped her ease down on the couch.

He wasn't smiling. "What's wrong with your knees?"

She shrugged. "I must've bruised them when I fell tonight."

"Do you need to go to the hospital?"

Maddie shook her head.

He pulled a cell phone from inside his suit coat. "I'm calling my car. You need—"

"No."

"Madison, be realistic. You need to be checked out."

"No, I don't. It's just my knees."

"Fine." He put it away. "Are they swollen?"

"Probably."

"Probably? Haven't you looked?"

"No, not really. I didn't want to look at the dance, and then Brian and Sherri were here...and after they left all I wanted to do was lay down."

"Let's see."

"What? No, they'll be fine."

"Madison, give me a break. They're not fine, or you wouldn't be hobbling around."

She sighed and lifted the edge of her nightgown to expose her knees. Both were puffy with swelling and a light shade of purple from bruising.

"Dammit, Madison, why didn't you say something?" Ring slipped off his suit coat and rolled up his shirt sleeves. "Lay back on the couch. Do you have an ice pack?"

"I have one here somewhere." She dug around the sofa. "Here it is."

"Good, you need to elevate your knees." He helped her lay down, grabbed a couple of pillows off the chair and arranged them underneath her knees. "Do you have a heating pad?"

"Yes, but this isn't necessary."

"Where?"

"Under the sink in the bathroom off the kitchen."

He was back in a minute. "Okay, we need to alternate, ice and heat. That'll help take the swelling down."

"How do you know about this? Did you play a doctor once?"

"Very funny." He shook his head. "My masseuse. She's used it in the past."

"You have a masseuse?"

He shrugged and nodded. "Are you allowed to take anything for the pain?"

"There's some stuff in the medicine cabinet the doctor said I could take."

He brought her back two tablets and a glass of water. Half an hour later, after the pain reliever and a round of ice and heat, Maddie had to admit it was working, the pain had lessened in her knees. Of course, she hadn't moved either.

"Here you go."

She scooted up a little on the couch and took the cup of tea. "Thanks."

"You're welcome. Back to ice now." He laid a new ice pack against her knees.

"Are you having tea too?"

"Nope, but a stiff drink wouldn't be amiss."

"Sorry." Maddie studied the flames for a moment. *This is so surreal.* Here she sat in her old nightgown with her fancy hair style all rumpled, very pregnant, in front of a man she hardly knew, and a famous man at that, and she didn't feel all that uncomfortable. *Weird.* She sat the mug on the coffee table, leaned back and closed her eyes.

"Better?" He slid into the chair across from her.

"Hmmm. Much better. Thanks for your help."

"No problem. Are you sure you shouldn't go to the hospital?" She nodded.

"What's the deal with that guy, anyway?"

"Fred? There's no deal, he's just—Fred. When I was little he used to come and play with my brother, or they'd be out in the wood shop with my father. A few years later, Josh moved onto junior high, but Fred struggled and had to repeat grades. One year, he and I were in the same class, and then I moved on too. The next year he just stopped going, and nobody could make him, no matter the threat."

"No offense, but I think he needs to be some place."

"He is some place...Northam."

Ring shook his head. "No, I mean like a school or a group home, where he can learn some kind of skills."

"Fred Edgars has plenty of skills. He is a major contributor in keeping his family's dairy farm going. He works from sunup to sundown, and often long after. He's very knowledgeable about animals, machinery, all aspects of farming. He's also a skilled woodworker. If he wasn't working on the farm, he was here, hanging out with my dad in the shop."

"Maybe so, but what happened tonight—"

"What happened tonight was an accident. Fred would never hurt me."

"Okay, if you say so...but could you do me a favor and stick to a waltz when it comes to dancing with him?"

Maddie laughed. "Fred doesn't waltz. He can't seem to get the timing. Everyone tried to teach him—his mother and sister, me, even my mom tried. My poor mom, Fred stepped on her foot and broke three of her toes. That year she didn't dance at the Harvest Ball at all. In fact, she had to wear a bedroom slipper for several months. But she was such a good sport, she sewed up a slipper in every color to wear with all her outfits. She even made a special one for Christmas day. It was red velvet. The top was edged with white lace and satin ribbons that held two of the tiniest bells I'd ever seen. They made a lovely jingle every time she took a step..." Maddie trailed off, her eyes on the fire, quiet for several moments. "Wow, I hadn't thought of that for years."

"You miss your parents a lot, don't you?"

She nodded. "Sometimes more than others. The holidays are hard."

"Is that their picture on the mantle?"

Madison glanced up. "Yes, the one on the left was on their wedding day. The one in the middle is all of us, it was taken at Christmas my senior year of high school, I think. And the one on the right is my brother, Josh, at his college graduation."

"She was very attractive." Ring rose and went to study the pictures in the dim light. "You look just like her. Same auburn hair, same bone structure. They were a handsome couple."

"Thank you. People who knew her tell me that a lot. My parents met in college, but it was several years later before they dated. She was teaching Home Ec at Northam High and a coworker convinced her to go out on a blind date with a buddy of her fiancé, just home from the service."

"Your dad?"

Maddie nodded. "They'd gone to the same college, and as it turns out they'd been attracted to each other but were too shy to say anything. Not this time around. My mother told me they spent every available moment together, and still it wasn't enough time to share all they wanted to tell each other, so after six months they got married. You know, they always had a lot to share. I'd often find them at the table, their heads together, laughing about something."

He glanced at the group picture of her family. "Nice hairdo."

"Thanks so much—what can I say? It was the "in" look that year. In Northam, at least."

"Still a nice looking family though."

"Thanks, I think so."

He shifted the picture of her brother. "You two have the same smile."

Maddie nodded. "He was so much fun."

Neither of them said anything for a few minutes. Ring moved to the couch and pulled the ice pack off her knees. "I think the swelling is actually going down a little, but they're going to be black and blue."

Maddie shrugged. "It's not like I'm going to be wearing a mini-skirt anytime soon, pregnant or not."

"How do they feel?"

"Stiff."

"Where's your bedroom? Upstairs?"

She nodded. "I was actually contemplating sleeping right here when you knocked."

"Are you going to be comfortable there?"

"Probably not. I have a bigger pillow I've taken to sleeping with upstairs on my bed."

"Let's get you up there then."

"No, that's okay. I can make it." For some reason, the thought of him seeing the upstairs and her bedroom felt too intimate. "You don't have to help."

"I'm helping. I don't want you falling down the stairs and hurting yourself."

Maddie made to rise, and Ring slid an arm around her as they worked their way to the staircase. She rested a hand on the wide balustrade. For the first time since she was about five, it looked like a long way up.

"Do you want me to carry you?"

"I don't think so, He-Man. No sense in both of us falling down the stairs." She lifted her foot to the first step. Ring's grip on her tightened. Maddie tried to ignore the fiery pain of protest in her knee as she put weight on it. Her knee won. She set her foot on the floor again.

"Are you sure you don't want me to—"

"No, just give me a minute. Please." She studied the stairs for a moment. "I've got it. The first few days after my Mom broke her toes, she'd sit on her bottom and scoot up the stairs when it was time to go to bed. I bet that'd work." Ring let go of her, but hovered as she turned and eased herself onto the step. Taking a deep breath, Maddie put the heels of her hands flat on the stair tread above and pushed. It took two tries to get the next step. "Whew. This isn't as easy as you'd think with this." She pointed to her abdomen. Not to mention her knees screamed in protest as she'd used them to help lever herself upward. *I can do this.*

"Madison, are you sure? I can get you up the stairs." His gaze was level with hers. "I promise I won't drop you."

Maddie shook her head. "No, this will work. It'll just take a few minutes." Nearing the top of the steps, she could feel the flannel of her nightgown sticking to her back with perspiration. She ignored it and the throbbing in her knees. One thing she couldn't ignore was Ring's close proximity as he moved up the steps with her, one at a time. *He smells good.* She flushed. *What are you thinking? You're as big as a house and all you can think about is how he smells? Pregnancy hormones, no doubt.*

"Are you okay? Do you need to rest? Your face is red."

*Oh, great. Get a move on. One more step.* In her hurry, Maddie caught her hand on the stair runner. The sudden jerk to a stop threw her off balance, and she toppled forward. She put her hands out to stop herself, but Ring was already there to catch her. His arms went around her, and he held her weight easily. Madison grasped at him in an automatic reflex and got an even more intense whiff of his scent as her face pressed against his shirt collar and the warm skin of his neck. Her indrawn breath brought the slightly salty taste of his skin to her lips.

"Are you okay?" He whispered near her ear.

Neither of them moved.

She gave a nod.

He shifted and slid his arm under her injured knees, lifting her off the last step to the landing.

Maddie kept her arms around his neck and her face buried. *He feels so good. I just want to enjoy this nearness for a moment.*

Ring stepped into the first room to the right.

"Madison, where's your room?"

His voice was still a whisper. Maddie lifted her head with reluctance. The night light showed they stood in the small room she'd decorated as a nursery. "You can go right through that door."

He carried her through the doorway at the end of the room into a much larger bedroom, dimly illuminated by the light from a lamp on the landing. Maddie relinquished her grip as he sat her on a bench at the foot of a large four-poster bed. He turned down the bedding before scooping her up again to deposit her on the cool sheets. He tugged the quilt over her.

"Better?"

"Yes. Thank you."

They were both whispering now, but it felt right.

"It's chilly in here. Are you warm enough?"

"I'm okay. I lit the fire earlier, but I haven't had a chance to put more wood in."

Ring went to the brick hearth across the room. In a couple of minutes, the banked embers went from a glow to a flame as he added a few small sticks of dry birch. The light from the fire cast the room in flickering shadows as he neared the bed again.

"Where's your special pillow?"

"Over in that chair."

Ring retrieved it and Maddie rolled onto her side and flipped the bedding back. She took care in tucking the pillow between her bruised knees, before using it as a cushion for her stomach. She pulled it close to her chest as she wrapped her arms around it, aware Ring watched her movements. The pillow, meant to ease the discomfort of pregnancy often eased the discomfort of loneliness as she clung to it in a nightly ritual. Not tonight.

Ring tugged the quilt back over her. "Are you warmer?"

His actions brought sudden tears to her eyes. *How long has it been since someone had asked if I was warm enough?* A very long time. She nodded, but was unable to hide the sudden sob that caught in her throat.

"Madison? Are you okay? What's wrong?"

She felt the mattress sink under his weight as he climbed onto the bed. "Madison?"

Tears streamed down her face.

"Madison? Talk to me. Where does it hurt?"

Panic was clear in his voice. She gulped, unable to stop the tears. "In my heart." Madison let go and sobbed out loud. "I miss my family."

He kicked off his shoes and slid over next to her, wrapping her in his arms. He smoothed her hair back off her face and let her cry.

Maddie drew a shuddering breath. "Sorry," she whispered against the wet front of his shirt.

He continued to stroke her hair. "Nothing to be sorry about."

"I don't know what came over me. But thank you for listening and being here...and for being you."

He gave her a little squeeze and planted a kiss on the top of her head. "No, thank you. Do you know how long it's been since someone's needed me just for me, without an ulterior motive? A long time."

"You're kidding, right? You're Ring Stanford. You must have lots of friends."

He shook his head. "I have acquaintances. No close friends."

"What? Not even from when you were growing up? School friends?"

"I didn't go to regular school...I spent most of my time on a movie set."

"I don't know much about Hollywood and all that, but I do know there are laws about child actors getting an education. Didn't you have a tutor?"

"Yes, several in fact. But they spent most of my class time reviewing the curriculum with my agent."

His emphasis on curriculum held a derisive tone. "Wait, didn't you tell me your father was your agent?"

He nodded. "The studio pressured him to hire a tutor, and I was excited when he told me he'd found someone. I got schooled all right—when I walked in on them a week after she arrived."

"How old were you?"

"Ten."

*Ten?* "What'd you do?"

"I told him I was going to tell my mother."

"Did you?"

"No. My father could be very persuasive when he wanted to be—without leaving any marks. A little trick he'd learned as a minister to keep his followers in line. He used it on my mother and me whenever he felt it was necessary."

Madison didn't move. *Is he serious?* "What'd you do?"

"Nothing. I schooled myself as much as possible in the time allotted. There were several more tutors over the years, each one younger than the one before, and all demanding more money, more perks—jewelry, cars, the usual stuff. The last one was only a year older than I was at the time." He leaned his head against the headboard and let out a deep sigh. "Destiny. Well, her real name was Nancy, but she wanted to be an actress. Who didn't? We spent a lot of time together. She was my first..." He stopped. "Anyway, I was half in love with her myself. She's the one that clued me into what was really going on."

"What do you mean?"

"My father had picked up a drug habit somewhere along the way, and what money he wasn't spending on women, cars, whatever, went to drugs. My money."

"What happened?"

"I'd had enough. Another child actor had just won emancipation from his parents, so I went to the same lawyer and filed papers against my father. I tried to talk Nancy into coming with me, but she wouldn't. She told me I was a kid and couldn't do anything. She was afraid of my father's beatings, but the truth is, I think she was more afraid of not knowing where her next fix was coming from."

"What about your mother? Did she ever find out?"

He nodded. "Eventually. I knew as soon as my father got served the papers, he'd be looking for me. With the help of the lawyer, I laid low and waited. He hunted for me for weeks and then just stopped. Several days went by, and no one had seen him or Nancy. Then the lawyer showed up with an opened envelope the cops had found in Nancy's apartment. It was a birthday card from Nancy. She'd written a note inside."

Ring was back to stroking Maddie's hair in an absent manner.

"I'm going to take care of your old man, so he won't hassle you no more. Then I have to check out too. I'm knocked up, and I wish it was yours, but I'm sure it's not. Destiny."

A shiver ran through Maddie's body.

"She shot him up with an overdose and then herself." Ring gave a harsh laugh. "You want to know the funny thing? The lawyer delivered the card on my eighteenth birthday. Talk about irony."

"Ring, I'm sorry."

"Me too." He leaned his head back again, and Maddie watched the movement of his Adam's apple as he swallowed. "Wow. I haven't thought of that in a while, and besides my mother, you're the only person I've ever told."

"I'll never tell anyone."

"I know that." He stopped stroking her hair. "How are you feeling?"

"Right now? Pretty comfortable."

"Good. I need to put some more wood on the fire."

Maddie raised her head, and he slid off the bed. She watched him add wood and studied his outline in the flare up of the flames.

He came back and stretched out next to her on his stomach. "This really is a great house."

Maddie smiled. "Thanks. Some people might not agree with you. It can be really hard to heat as you can see."

"It'd be nothing to put a new heating system in. But look at this room. Huge windows, braided rugs... a fireplace. The heating bill is nothing compared to what you'd pay to try and replicate it. You were lucky to grow up in a house like this."

"I was."

He pulled a pillow over and folded it in half, resting his head on it. "Tell me about it."

So she did. About the time Josh had saved her when they slid down the banister. She lost her grip. He'd pushed her back onto the stairs, even as he'd toppled over the side and broke his arm. She told Ring about her mother teaching her to cook and sew. About community work, family dinners and holidays, especially Christmas. Her mother decorated, inside and out. Garlands, lights and a huge tree in the parlor downstairs for their annual Christmas party. They made holiday baskets for families and caroled at the local nursing home. Maddie told him about these traditions and more until long into the night.

# Chapter 9

Maddie fought her way to consciousness, groaning at the pain as she moved her legs under the sheet. She ran her tongue over dry lips and yawned before opening her eyes. The mound of her belly was her first sight, as well as the masculine arm looped over it. She froze. Individual muscles moved under dark skin as the arm tightened and Ring Stanford moved closer to her on the bed, his eyes closed, his breathing even, the only thing between them the blankets. *He's probably freezing.* Maddie couldn't quite see her breath, but the room was cold. The fire had to be embers by now. *I should turn up the thermostat.* "Ring?"

His eyes opened and he stared at her, his gaze disoriented for a moment. He closed and opened them again. "Morning."

"Morning."

"I guess we fell asleep."

She nodded.

He shivered. "You're right. It does get cold in here. Of course, it doesn't help I've been waking up in Mexico for how many months now?" He gave her a lazy smile, but it was cut short by another shiver. "I can fix this."

Maddie pushed herself into a sitting position and watched his efficient movements. The room was already warming as he neared the bed again.

"How are your knees this morning?"

Maddie moved her legs under the sheet and gave a small grimace. "Sore, but they don't feel as stiff. Let's see." She tossed the blankets aside and swung her legs to the floor. "So far, so good." He was at her elbow as she used the mattress to steady herself. "I'm good." She took a halting step and then another, reaching for the door casing. "I'm good. Really." She put a hand up when he made to follow her. "I'll be right back. I'm just going to the bathroom across the hall." A few steps later she closed the bathroom door and a few minutes after that she stood in front of the sink washing her hands. Glancing in the mirror, Maddie was startled by the reflection. The intricate cap of braids Sherri had done was sagging on one side, while on the other side several braids stood up in loops, somehow teased out of the weave to stand alone.

"Well, good morning, Medusa," Madison muttered, her face turning a bright red. "I bet that's not something Ring Stanford's used to seeing in the morning." She groaned and worked her fingers through the braids at the back of her head. After two tangles she realized this was going to take a few minutes. *I need to sit down.* She'd closed the lid on the toilet and sat down when there was a light tap on the door.

"Are you okay?"

Madison could hear the hesitancy in his voice. *Has he been standing out there all this time?* "I'm fine." She didn't hear any footsteps. "Listen, would you mind putting on the tea kettle? I'm going to get dressed. There's linen in the downstairs bath if you'd like to shower or freshen up." Still no footsteps. "I'll call you when I'm ready to come downstairs." Nothing. "Ring?"

"What?"

"I'm fine. I'll call you. Okay?"

There was silence for a few moments before she heard a quiet "Okay," and receding footfalls. She relaxed and went to work on her hair.

It was twenty minutes before Maddie stood at the top of the stairs listening to him move around below. She'd decided to forego standing in the shower this morning. She slipped on a long sleeve pullover and plaid wool maternity jumper. Her hair was kinked from braiding it while wet, but there wasn't much she could do about that right now. She made another attempt at smoothing it down.

Ring appeared at the foot of the stairs and smiled up at her. He had showered, his hair still wet. He hustled up the steps. "Are you ready?"

As he towered over her, Madison was enveloped by the smell of shampoo, soap and something else. *Toast?* "Are you cooking?"

He nodded. "Since you don't have a cook, I'm giving it a try. It's not much, but I thought it'd get you started on the day."

*He's making me breakfast?*

"How do you want to do this? Sitting down again?"

Maddie shook her head. "I think I can make it on my feet. I'd like to try."

"Are you sure?"

She nodded and edged to the railing. "Why don't you go in front of me, just in case?" The trip down the stairs was slow and painful, but manageable at least. "Whew. Good. That's better." He continued to hover. "I'm fine, really. Just sore."

"Why don't you sit here? I got the fire going again. I'll be right back."

Maddie was settled on the sofa when he came back in with a tray and set it down. "Here you go." Orange juice, tea and some kind of breakfast sandwich made with a slightly burned English muffin. "Sorry, I overcooked the bread. I'm not much good with a toaster."

"No, that's fine." She picked up the cup of tea and took a sip. The warmth of the liquid relaxed her from the inside out.

"Are you going to try the sandwich?"

"What? Oh, yes, of course." She picked up the plate and took a small bite, the crunch of the crisp bread loud inside her head as she chewed. He watched her, an expectant expression plain on his face. She nodded, chewed some more, took a sip of tea and swallowed. "Very good."

He broke out in a smile. "Good. My chef sometimes makes them if I'm home on the weekend, so I took a shot at it. I thought it was important you have a good breakfast, with the baby and all..." he trailed off.

She smiled back. "Thanks."

They sat smiling at each other a few moments before he cleared his throat and rose. "I've called my car; it should be here in a few minutes. Are you going to be okay?"

She nodded, and still he didn't move.

"Where are you going?" The words were out her mouth before she had time to think. "Ah, what I mean is—not now, but ahh, over the holiday."

"Actually, I'm going to my mother's in Jersey to spend a couple of days with her. I haven't visited in a while, so it'll be nice to see her. Plus, I need to tell her about the baby."

"What? Do you think it's fair to spring it on her? What will she think?"

"Are you kidding? She'll be thrilled."

Maddie's thoughts must have shown on her face.

"She will, really. She'll be bragging about it at the next mahjong game."

Maddie shook her head. "I think you should wait to tell her until after the baby is born."

"Why?"

"Well..." Maddie studied the arm of the sofa. "What if she tells people and then someone talks to—I don't know, someone else and it gets to someone it shouldn't and gets out? Then what?"

"Don't worry about it. Nothing will happen. I'll ask her to keep it quiet. She won't like it, but she'll do it."

His eyes were on her, but Maddie couldn't meet his gaze.

"Madison?" He crossed the room and sat on the sofa next to her. "Tell me what you're thinking."

She lifted her eyes to meet his intense scrutiny, concern evident in his expression. "This whole thing is so crazy. All I wanted to do was live a quiet life and raise my baby. I'm afraid, sooner or later, the Dr. Carson scandal is going to come out, as well as the fact I got fired because of it. And as much as I don't want to, I'll live with it and in a year or so, it'll die down. But if it ever comes out you're the baby's father, it'll be the closest Northam ever comes to a celebrity. The gossips will never let it go...I can deal with it, but what about the baby? That's not fair. I'd have to move." She glanced around the room. "Northam and this house are the only home I've ever known. I don't want to leave." Tears welled. Madison wiped her eyes on the sleeve of her shirt. "Darn pregnancy hormones."

"Madison, I'll do everything I can to make sure this stays quiet until we can figure out what to do about the situation."

"What about next week? Maybe it's not such a good idea to go."

"Next week is all set. It's very private. We'll be staying in the same compound, but separate houses. It'll be good for you. You need a break. Trust me. Okay?"

Maddie sniffed and nodded.

He slipped a finger under her chin and lifted her face to meet his eyes again. "Okay?"

Maddie exhaled in a small gust. "Okay."

"Good." He smiled. "I think you're the first woman I've ever run across that doesn't want to be seen with me. Not much of an ego boost." He was still holding her face in his hand and leaned forward to give her a quick kiss on the cheek. "I've got to go before the whole neighborhood is awake. I'll call you tonight."

Maddie sat on the couch long after she heard the back door close. *Ring Stanford just kissed me.*

# Chapter 10

"I can't believe we're leaving in the morning." Sherri refilled her wine glass.

Madison covered the leftover stuffing and opened the refrigerator. "Where am I supposed to fit this?"

"Hold on." Sherri set her glass down and shuffled several bowls around inside the fridge before taking the small pan from Maddie and sliding it onto a shelf. It took two tries to close the door. "Brian, you'd better eat up these leftovers before you start on anything else. And I don't mean just Maddie's pie. Turkey too."

"I will. I will." Brian shook his head. "Man, you're such a nag."

"Am not." Sherri scooped up her glass. "I've got to finish packing."

"Your car should be warmed up. Are you all set?" Brian held up Maddie's coat.

"Sure. Thanks for having me over. It was great. See you in the morning?" she called to Sherri.

"Of course it was great, you cooked it. I'll be ready by 7:00 sharp," Sherri answered from the living room. "Happy Thanksgiving."

Brian opened the car door and then closed it again before Madison could get in. "Are you sure this is a good idea? Maybe I should go with you girls...I've heard Mexico can be a dangerous place."

"Brian, we'll be fine." Madison patted her abdomen. "How much trouble can I get into lugging this around? Besides, to tell you the truth, I could use a break. A lot of stuff has gone on around here lately, and it'll be nice to get away for a few days before the Christmas rush." That much was definitely not a lie.

Brian nodded. "That's true. At least that Stanford guy left. I don't buy the looking at real estate story. We're a little town with plain everyday folks. Nothing here for the big time Hollywood type. Why was he here, really?"

Maddie shrugged.

"And what did he want with you?"

She shrugged again. "Does it matter? He's gone now. I'd better get going...early day tomorrow." Madison gave his arm a squeeze. "I'll bring you back a great souvenir. Happy Thanksgiving." He pulled the car door open and she climbed in. She waved good bye and pulled out of the driveway.

Sleep didn't come easily that night though; Brian's words kept coming back to her. *We are plain everyday people, what do we—I have in common with Ring Stanford? I've been on a red carpet, but not the red carpet. I hate having my picture taken. I've been known to clip coupons...I bet Ring Stanford's wife never clipped coupons.* That was another whole issue—Anne Reese Miller. They were still married, so technically Mrs. Ring Stanford.

When the alarm went off the next morning, Madison wanted to pull the blankets up over her head. Crawling out of bed, she showered, had her tea and was in the car Ring arranged sitting in the Holts' driveway by 6:45. Sherri had her suitcases lined up on the porch—all five of them. She lugged one down the steps as the driver opened the trunk and met her halfway up the walkway. "I'll take that, miss. Why don't you join Ms. O'Neill in the car?"

"Ah, thank you." Sherri slid onto the seat next to Madison. "You hired a driver? Wow, you're really going first class."

After another trip to the porch, the driver slid in behind the wheel and lowered the glass partition between the front and back. "Are you ladies all set?"

At Madison's nod, the glass slid silently back in place and soon they were headed south on Interstate 91.

"Sherri, what's in all those suitcases?"

"You know...lots of new dresses, shoes to match. Shorts. Three or four bathing suits. Make up. Nail polish. Oh yeah, my blow dryers and curling irons. Let's see...what else?"

"You brought more than one blow dryer and curling iron?"

"I had to. As backup, in case one broke."

"You're on vacation. Are you really going to worry about curling your hair?"

"Of course. Being on vacation is all the more reason to be looking good. You never know who you're going to meet. Maybe I'll have a little vacation romance."

"Anything's possible." Now that the time had come to tell Sherri the purpose for the trip, Maddie wasn't sure how her friend would take it. "Ahh, there are a couple of details I need to tell you about the trip."

"More details? Maddie, it isn't like you to leave out details. What's going on?"

Maddie finished explaining as they pulled up in front of the terminal at the airport.

"Let me get this straight...we're flying out of Lebanon, New Hampshire, not Boston? In Ring Stanford's private jet? We're staying in adjoining houses, but no one will know we're all together?"

Maddie nodded and opened her purse, handing Sherri an envelope.

"What's this?" Sherri opened the envelope. "Money? For what?"

"It's the money you gave me toward the vacation."

"What? Why?" Sherri paused. "Is he paying for all of this?"

Maddie nodded. "Otherwise, he threatened to buy the Cohen place."

"Holy crap. You're kidding? He would've really bought it?"

Maddie nodded again.

"Wow."

"Are you upset?"

"Are you kidding? This is great." Sherri was silent for a moment. "I have to ask you something though."

Maddie waited.

"Why? Why is he paying for all of this? What's going on?"

Maddie cleared her throat. "He wants us to get to know each other better."

"What? Ring Stanford has the hots for you?"

"Well, you don't have to sound so shocked."

"No, no...that's not it. You just don't seem like his type. It doesn't add up."

"That's because there's more," Maddie said in a quiet voice. "It's his baby I'm carrying."

Sherri opened and closed her mouth without uttering a word. Three times. "What?" The word reverberated around the inside of the car. "What? Are you freakin' kiddin' me? Was he on the doctor's special list?"

"It seems so. Dr. Carson probably thought he was returning a favor. His daughter was bipolar. I used to watch out for her at school." Maddie shook her head. "This is all so crazy, I can hardly believe it myself, but Ring claims to want to be a part of the baby's life."

"Wow. Wow. Wow. You're going to be famous. I can't wait to tell—"

"No, you can't tell anyone. I don't want anyone to know. You have to promise not to say a word to anyone, not even Brian. I mean it, Sherri."

"Okay, okay. I won't, I promise. But Maddie, how long do you think you're going to be able to keep this a secret?"

"Forever, I hope."

Sherri rolled her eyes. "Not likely."

"I don't want to talk about this anymore right now. Let's get going, okay?"

"Sure. That's fine with me."

The driver unloaded their luggage. Once they identified themselves, everything was taken care of. It was hard to believe by the afternoon they'd left the chilly weather of New England behind as they stepped away from the customs officer who greeted them as they exited the plane in Cancun.

A man in a black suit stepped up. "*Señorita* O'Neill?"

Madison nodded.

"I'm Carlos, your driver. This way, please." He led the women to a limo sitting on the edge of the tarmac and opened the back door. "If you'll be seated, it will take me just a moment to gather your luggage." They climbed in, and he closed the door.

"Will you look at this?" Sherri gasped. "Champagne and strawberries? Are you kidding?" She shifted on the seat. "Look—a phone and a TV? A bar? What's this?" She pulled open a small compartment. "Holy smokes! It's a wet bar. Water, soda, cheese, nuts. You want something?"

"No, thanks."

"Do you think I'll have time for some champagne?"

Maddie glanced out the window. Carlos had picked up two of Sherri's suitcases and managed several steps before setting them down again. He pulled out a handkerchief and swiped at his brow, tucked it away, exhaled and lifted the bags to stagger toward the car. "Oh, yes. Plenty of time."

An hour later, the limo glided through wrought iron gates surrounded by high stucco walls. A large marble fountain stood at the center of the drive. Carlos parked the car and opened Maddie's door. "Here you are."

Maddie and Sherri exited. Two huge identical houses edged the circular drive separated by wide expenses of green lawn and palm trees as well as several vibrant flower gardens.

"Carlos, which one are we staying in?"

The chauffeur shrugged at Madison's question. "I don't know."

They turned at the sound of a closing door. A woman with a basket over her arm came down the walkway of the closest house.

"Hold on, I'll find out." Carlos headed toward the woman. *"Hola, Señora. Un momento, por favor."* They held a lively discussion for several minutes. She left as he came back to where they stood.

"Okay, that's Rosa. She's going to be one of your housekeepers. She thinks you're staying in the house she just came out of. I'll get your bags."

"We have more than one housekeeper? Never mind." Madison pulled several bills out of her purse and held them out. "Thank you, Carlos."

He shook his head as he lifted a suitcase out of the trunk. "The tip's already been paid—a real good one too."

Madison tucked the money away. "Thank you for your help."

"Sure." He reached inside his coat. "Here's my card. You need anything while you're here—you call me. I'll take care of it."

"Thank you, Carlos."

The large, airy house had more glass and marble than Madison had ever seen in one place. She stood looking around in disbelief.

Sherri glanced into several rooms. "Bedrooms." She pounded up the stairs only to return a few minutes later. "You are not going to believe it. There are more bedrooms up there. There's also a home theater and a game room. I wonder what else is here." She hurried toward the back of the house.

Carlos brought in luggage. "Where would you like these?"

"Oh, mine is the black one." Madison stepped through the closest doorway. A large bed covered in white linens occupied one wall. Floor to ceiling glass panels comprised the outside wall. Several of the panels were open to the breeze and led to a covered porch with a chaise lounge, a small table and two chairs. Beyond that, flower gardens and then the beach completed the scenery. *What a great place to read or just relax.* "Carlos, you can put my luggage in here."

He went to get another load when Sherri appeared. "This place is incredible. I checked out back. Besides the beach, there's a swimming pool, a hot tub and a tennis court. And I'm not sure, but I think there's a helicopter landing pad too." She pointed to Maddie's suitcase. "Are you taking this room? There are bigger bedrooms upstairs with great views."

Madison smiled. "I like this room."

"Excuse me. I believe this one is yours too." Carlos set Maddie's second suitcase down. "Can you tell me where the rest of it's going?"

Sherri gave him a sheepish smile. "Those are all mine." She turned to Madison. "Do you want me to take a room downstairs?"

"No, I'm fine."

"Great!" She beckoned the man with a wave of her hand. "I'll show you."

Carlos followed her, closing the door behind him.

Madison unpacked and then stretched out on the chaise lounge to enjoy the view. Ten minutes later, a quick knock was followed by Sherri bursting through the door. "Can you believe this place?"

"It is beautiful." Maddie pushed herself into a sitting position. "I can hardly believe we're here."

"I can, and I don't want to waste a minute of it. Are you getting your suit on?"

Looking at Sherri in her micro bikini Maddie wasn't so sure she wanted to appear in a bathing suit. She rose from the chair, went to the closet and chose a sun dress instead, stepping into the bathroom to put it on. "Is there anyone else around?"

"I haven't seen anyone. Where's the new suit you bought?" Sherri asked when Madison reappeared. "It's really cute."

"I don't feel like swimming right now. I think I'll just go wading."

"C'mon. Who's going to see you? There's not a soul out there."

"Maybe later."

"Okay. But you've got to see this place. C'mon."

They walked across the hot sand of the deserted beach. The lighter azure blue of the ocean competed with the azure blue of the cloudless sky for beauty. The water splashed with gentle warmth around their ankles.

"Wow. This is great." Sherri continued to move deeper until she was in up past her waist. She ducked down into the water. "This water is so warm. Why don't you get your suit on?"

Maddie shook her head, but hiked her dress up and waded a little deeper into the water. "It is nice."

"Nice? It's gorgeous."

Sherri swam for a while and Maddie splashed water on her arms to cool off before working her way back to shore. "I think I'm going to need to get out of the sun for a while. I don't want to burn."

They returned to the house.

"I'm going to change; I'll be right back." Sherri headed up the stairs.

Maddie was about to follow her when the telephone rang. Not sure what to do, Maddie picked it up. "Hello?"

"Hi. It's Ring. I'm checking in to make sure you made it and are settling in okay."

"We're fine. This is a great house; you must hate to leave."

"I haven't actually been there yet. By the time we get done for the day all I want to do is crash. I have a trailer here on the set. It looks like it's one of those days. I'm not sure I'm going to make it there today."

"That's okay."

"Not really. We're using this time to get to know each other, remember?"

"Yes, I know, but if you're busy..." Maddie left the statement unfinished.

"Today, yes—tomorrow probably, but we're almost done, so I should be free in a few days for sure. Do you need anything? Dave will be by there later to check on you and bring out some of our stuff."

"No, I can't think of anything. Wait, can you tell me where there's a grocery store? We'll need to buy some food. Do you think Dave would mind taking us when he stops by?"

"Sure. Was there something in particular? There's supposed to be food there. Did you check?"

"No." She walked into the airy kitchen, the tile floor cool beneath her bare feet and pulled opened one of the doors of the stainless steel refrigerator that stretched the length of the wall. Beverages of every kind lined up in neat rows covered the shelves. The next compartment was loaded with prepared food. At the front, there was fresh salsa, as well as large platters arranged with fruit, several salads, cold chicken and poached salmon. "The refrigerator's full and it looks like someone made food. Who did that?"

"I assume it's the cook Dave hired. He's ready to go home, and said he'll only stay if we hire a cook. She was supposed to come in and make a light lunch and then come back later to make dinner."

"A light lunch? She made enough food to feed an army. We won't need her to come back and make dinner, that's for sure."

"Okay. I'll let Dave know. I'm being paged back to the set. We'll talk later?"

"Sure."

"Listen, Dave should be there soon. He's going to be staying at night, at least until I'm done here. If you need anything, he'll be right next door. Okay?"

"Okay."

"I'll talk to you soon. I'm looking forward to seeing you. Bye, Madison."

"Bye." She hung up the phone.

"Ta-da...what do you think?"

Maddie looked up. Sherri was back, her hair windblown, dressed in a form-fitting tropical print sheath, but still barefoot. The short dress accentuated her long tan legs "You look like Tarzan's Jane. It's a good look for you."

Sherri grinned. "Thanks. I'm starved after that swim. Maybe we should go out and find some food before it gets dark?"

Maddie opened the refrigerator door again. "Ta-da."

"Holy cow. This is all for us? Where'd it come from?"

"Evidently, Dave hired someone to cook."

"Dave who?"

"He's Ring's manager."

Sherri reached in, plucked a slice of watermelon off one of the platters and took a bite. "Mmm, this is good. Really good."

They pulled several platters out of the fridge and had no more than finished setting the table on the shaded porch facing the ocean than there was a knock at the front door.

"Who could that be? The front gate is locked."

Sherri shrugged. "One way to find out." It was several moments before she returned. "We have company. Dave Martinez?" She raised her eyebrows a couple of times and smiled at Maddie before stepping aside.

*Ring's manager.* "Mr. Martinez? It's nice to finally meet you." Maddie came forward.

"Nice to meet you too." The swarthy man was dressed in a polo shirt and shorts.

Maddie nodded. "Please sit down. Can I get you something to drink?"

"You don't have to do that. I just wanted to let you know I'm next door."

"We insist. What can we get you?"

*Sherri insists?* "Mr. Martinez, this is my friend, Sherri Holt."

He extended his hand and Sherri gave him a radiant smile. "It's a pleasure, Mr. Martinez."

He smiled back. "The pleasure's mine. And call me Dave."

"Okay, Dave it is." The two continued to smile at each other.

Maddie cleared her throat. "Dave, would you like to join us for an early dinner? There's more food than we can begin to eat."

"Are you sure you don't mind?"

"Not at all," Sherri piped in and gave him another smile.

He nodded. "Great. Give me a few minutes to settle in, and I'll be back."

After he left, Madison went into the kitchen for another plate and silverware with Sherri hot on her heels. "That's Ring Stanford's manager? What's the deal with him?"

"What do you mean?"

"Is he single? Married?"

"I have no idea. Why?"

Sherri shrugged. "No reason. I was just wondering."

It didn't take Maddie long to figure out Sherri was more than curious when it came to Ring Stanford's manager. He arrived back in less than a half hour, freshly shaved, dressed in light pants and a white shirt, open at the throat. Dave volunteered to make a pitcher of some rum-laced tropical drink and throughout dinner, he regaled them with stories of celebrity life.

"Aha." Sherri hooted and slapped her palm on the table, several glasses of punch later. "I read about that in *Hot Hollywood*. See, Maddie, I told you those stories are true." She took another sip of the punch. "I knew it." She relaxed in her chair and tipped her head back, her smile wide and her cheeks flushed.

"Are you okay?"

"Maddie, I couldn't be better. I feel so relaxed. This is great." Sherri leveled her gaze on Dave. "I think we should go for a walk along the beach. Would you like to go with us?"

He smiled. "Absolutely."

Maddie stifled a yawn behind her hand. "I'm sorry. I think the travel and the sun are catching up to me." She rose and picked up her plate. "Goodness, it's almost midnight. I'm going to turn in, but you two go ahead."

"Are you sure? Are you going to be all right?"

"Of course. I'm just tired. Tomorrow's another day. I'll see you in the morning." Maddie smiled to reassure her friend and headed to her room. Exhausted as she was, several hours later Maddie was still awake. She turned on the lamp to look at the small clock before her eyes touched on her cell phone on the night stand. She picked it up and pushed the button. "A text message? When?"

*Madison, on the set late. Will call you tomorrow.*

She typed a reply.

*I understand. Talk to you then.*

Maddie laid back down. A few seconds later her phone rang. "Hello?"

"Hi, it's me. Ring." He yawned. "What time is it?"

"Ahh—almost two o'clock."

"Why aren't you asleep?"

Madison rolled onto her side. "I don't know—I couldn't sleep."

"Why? Is something wrong?"

"No, not really."

He yawned again.

"I'll let you go back to sleep. I'm sorry."

"No, don't hang up. Please. I'm glad you texted. I thought of calling you earlier, but thought you'd be asleep."

Maddie could hear him shift around.

"Tell me what you did today."

"Well...we went swimming and then Dave came over for dinner." She smiled. "He was quite entertaining."

"Dave? Entertaining?"

"Yes. Then he and Sherri went for a walk."

"Really?" was all Ring said on the subject. "What else?"

"That's about it. How about you?"

"We shot until almost one, and then I came in here and crashed."

"Oh, my word. You just got to bed."

"No worries. I'm pushing to get done. I think we might be finished by tomorrow night."

It was Maddie's turn to yawn. "I'm sorry. I guess I'm sleepier than I realized." She rolled the other way. "I forgot my big pillow."

"We'll get you one. Try to get some sleep, okay? You need to rest."

"I will. Night, Ring."

"Night, Maddie."

# Chapter 11

For the next two days, Madison tried to content herself with the sun, surf and fresh food Rosa prepared. Dave Martinez made frequent visits, but no Ring. This morning, Dave had stopped by on his way to the location to tell her Ring was trying to finish up, but it might take another day or two. Maddie tamped down her disappointment.

Later that afternoon, she joined Sherri on the beach to stretch out in a chaise lounge at the water's edge. Fluffy clouds dotted the horizon, their white stark against the blue of the sky. Maddie inhaled and let out a long sigh. She closed her eyes.

Sherri turned to study her friend. "Are you okay?"

"Yes. I'm not used to lazing around."

"Thank goodness, I have no such problem." Sherri reclined her chair.

Neither woman said anything for a few minutes.

"He'll be here soon, you know. Dave told me he's working hard to get here."

Maddie nodded. "I know. I'm fine. How could I not be? It's beautiful here. It's just I'm bored."

"Bored? You're kidding?"

"No. With Rosa and Manuela doing all the housekeeping and cooking, there's nothing to do."

"What? Maddie, don't you think you should be resting? You're supposed to be on vacation, remember?"

"I know, but I've rested about as much as I can stand."

"Not me. This place is paradise, and the company's been great."

"Thanks." Maddie raised her eyebrows. "But I have a feeling you're talking about Dave—you really like him, don't you?"

Sherri adjusted her chair to a sitting position again and pushed her sunglasses atop her head. "I do. He's smart and sophisticated and sarcastic—all at once, but he can be kind too. He's everything I never knew I wanted. How could I? There's definitely nobody like him in Northam." Sherri smiled. "I bet he doesn't even own a flannel shirt."

Maddie smiled back. "He's a nice man. Have you two talked about after we leave here?"

"No. There's nothing to talk about. He'll go back to his life, and I'll go back to Beulah's Beauty Nook." Sadness permeated Sherri's words. "I'm not bringing it up. This is my first real vacation; the romance is a bonus—I'm not going to ruin it." She reached out a hand to Madison. "Besides, I'm here with my best friend, what more could I ask for?"

"Good attitude. Enjoy it, and wait to see what happens." Maddie gave Sherri's hand a reassuring squeeze. "I just had a thought. How about we go downtown one of these nights? We can do some shopping."

"Do you think it's safe?"

"Probably, but we could ask Dave to go with us."

Sherri smiled. "I like that idea, and I wanted to look for some new bracelets anyway."

"Good, and I promised Bri a souvenir." Maddie swung her legs over the side of the chair. "Well, I need some exercise. I'm going to take a swim. Do you want to join me?"

Sherri shaded her eyes. "No, thank you. How about I be the life guard?"

Maddie stepped to the water's edge and waved a hand without looking back. She waded out into the gentle waves. It was half an hour later before she rolled onto her back in exhaustion, her stomach protruding from the water as she drifted in the shallows near shore. A shadow blocked out the sun. "Don't worry, Sherri, I'm fine." Maddie huffed out between breaths. "I just have to catch my breath. I went a little longer than I planned, but it should help me sleep tonight."

"You haven't been sleeping?"

Maddie sat upright. Ring stood over her in the water, dressed in a white tee shirt and swimming trunks. "You're here. I thought you wouldn't be here for several days yet." Madison pushed her wet hair back. *Oh, great. He would have to show up now.* "Well, I guess I should go change."

"Why? Did you have something planned for this afternoon?"

*How about get out of the water without you getting a look at me in this bathing suit?* "No."

"Well, let me grab a quick swim, and we'll figure something out."

"You don't have to do that. Why don't you relax? I know you've been working long hours."

"I'm fine." He tossed his shirt on the sand and dove neatly into the slow curling waves.

The warm water lapped around her on its way to shore. *Here's your chance. Get out while he's gone.* But he was back in a matter of minutes. Though lean, Maddie watched muscles move under the skin of Ring's tanned torso as he raised his arms to finger-comb his wet hair back. Two small scars showed white above the waistband of his trunks.

"Do you need to rest a while longer?"

She shook her head. "No, I'm okay now."

"How's the baby?"

Ring's quiet words brought Maddie's head up. "Good." She put her hand on the bump of her abdomen above water. "Growing every day."

"Good." He smiled and held out a hand. "Are you ready?"

"Not really."

"Did you overdo it? If you need to rest a while longer, that's fine."

She shook her head. "No, I'm fine. It's just..." she trailed off.

"Just what?"

"Oh, brother." Maddie rolled her eyes. "I'm not feeling very attractive these days, especially in a bathing suit."

He stared at her for a moment. "You're serious, aren't you?"

She nodded.

"Madison, you look great. When I saw you today my first thought was pregnancy agrees with you." He offered his hand again. "Come on."

She blushed, but accepted his help to stand and didn't say anything when he continued to hold her hand as they worked their way up the beach to the house.

By the morning of their third day together they'd established, among other things, Madison liked her pizza with tomatoes and fresh basil; he liked his with meat and cheese. She liked British dramas; Ring liked action movies. She liked board games; he hated them. She'd seen several of his movies; he'd never seen any of them. She was an early riser, most times, he slept until noon, but they both liked the beach, dogs and anything with coconut in it.

"Thank you for getting up early and coming with me." Madison smiled up at him as they walked the beach, the water washing around their ankles.

"I can't remember the last time I was up this early—but it was worth it. That sunrise was amazing." He faced the breeze coming off the ocean and inhaled. "I have to admit, there's something about this time of day...it's quiet and fresh, like a new start? Do you know what I mean?"

She nodded. "It is. That's why I love getting up early." They strolled in silence for a few minutes. "And thanks for inviting us. Sherri is having the time of her life. She loves it here. She may be spoiled for life anywhere else."

"You're welcome, and what about you? Would you live here?"

"Well, I admit there's something very surreal, almost magical about this place, but no, I think not. I would miss Northam too much."

"What makes Northam so special?"

"Everything. The people are great, and there's always something going on."

"In Northam?"

She smiled at his incredulous tone. "Yes, in Northam. In fact, after the Harvest Ball, things get even busier."

"Really? Like what?"

"Well, besides all the community things going on, I have to get ready for the Christmas party and, of course, the holiday dinner."

"A holiday dinner? Where does this happen?"

"At my house. It's another tradition my mother started. On Christmas day, she always cooked a ton of food and whoever showed up was welcome. I do the same thing."

"That sounds like a lot of work. What do you do if no one shows up?"

Maddie shrugged. "I don't know. It's never happened. Different people have come over the years, but there are regulars. I can always count on Albie Norstock, Mrs. Richards, Miss Timmons, the librarian—well, not her anymore, she passed away last month. Generally, it's people without family around. Last year, Chief Lawson came as he'd just moved to town." She paused. "And me too, since I have no family."

Her words ended on a quiet note, her expression sad. Ring quelled the urge to put his arms around her. "You're a really good person, Madison O'Neill."

Maddie blushed. "And what about you? What do you do?"

"For Christmas?"

She nodded.

"Not much actually." He rubbed the back of his neck. "Most of the time I'm either filming or promoting a movie somewhere, so I give my mother and a few of her friends a holiday cruise every year. In the past, I've gone to parties, there are always parties."

"Well, that's good, right? I love Christmas parties. I'm sure your parties are much more sophisticated, but we have food, of course—and sometimes there's singing and games too."

*Oh, there are games all right, but none you'd be interested in.* Last Christmas, he'd made the party rounds with Dave. Liquor, drugs and eager company highlighted every stop. *No, Madison O'Neill wouldn't go for those kinds of parties.* "If I found myself without family on Christmas day, would I be welcome at your dinner?"

She nodded after a few moments. "Though I'd have to figure out how to explain you."

"What's to explain? I'm alone and looking for some cheer like everyone else around the table. Northam sounds like a nice place to live." He paused. "And raise children."

His words brought another smile to Maddie's upturned face. "It is."

He slipped an arm around her shoulders and gave her a light squeeze as they continued down the beach.

"There's never anyone out here."

"This whole stretch of beach goes with the compound. There's no one here but us."

"Good." She sighed. "You must think I'm paranoid, but I want to keep this quiet."

They approached the house.

"Madison, you have to prepare yourself; it may get out anyway."

"Not if we're careful. No one needs to know."

"But you have to be realistic." He stopped and turned to face her as his dark eyes locked with hers. "It could happen."

"No, it can't."

"It could." Ring leaned closer, his voice husky. "And to be truthful, I don't care if the world—"

A cry cut him off.

Madison glanced around Ring and gasped. "There's someone in the bushes over there."

Ring wheeled around while at the same time shielding Maddie. "Come out of there. Now. Before I come in after you." The shrubs shook violently for a moment.

"Oh no."

The warmth of her breath touched Ring's back at her whispered words.

The bushes rustled for several more moments.

"How'd you get in here? Who do you belong to?"

Maddie leaned out from behind him.

Two dark haired children, a boy and girl, stood in front of the hedge, alternating between stealing glances and studying their feet.

"Who are you?" Ring asked again.

The little girl burst into tears.

"Aww, sweetie, it's okay." Madison hurried over and knelt down to enfold the child in her arms, patting her back. "Shh. Shh.

It's okay. It's okay." Once the tears subsided, she brushed the girl's hair back. "There, that's better. Are you lost?"

"No, we're waiting for our mama."

Maddie turned to the boy. "Oh, good. Where's your mother?"

The boy pointed to the house.

"Your mom's in there?"

The boy nodded.

"Who's your mother?" This came from Ring.

"Rosa."

Ring disappeared into the house.

"Why are you out here?"

"We were supposed to sit on the bench out front and wait, but Julieta wouldn't listen to me."

"I see. Your name is Julieta? That's a beautiful name." Madison smiled. "I'm sure you meant to listen, but sometimes it's hard to sit still, isn't it?"

The girl nodded.

"But I was in charge."

"And doing a good job of it, I'm sure. What's your name?"

"Tomas."

"Well, Tomas, my name is Madison, and I'm pleased to meet you both."

Neither child answered, their gazes on something behind Maddie. She turned. Several platters of food were laid out on the table of the covered porch as well as a pitcher of orange juice. "Would you like some breakfast?"

"*Sí.*"

Julieta moved forward only to have Tomas lay a restraining hand on her arm. "No. Mama said to wait on the bench. We need to go back."

The girl's bottom lip quivered. "But I want—"

"*Lo siento.* I'm sorry, *Señorita* O'Neill." Rosa apologized as she came to a stop next to Madison. "I'm sorry they disturbed you."

"It's fine, Rosa. They're not disturbing anyone."

"My husband got a chance for extra work and couldn't pass it up." The woman pushed a stray strand of hair behind her ear. "And my mother is too ill to care for them."

"Nothing serious, I hope."

"Unfortunately, it is. Cancer." Tears stood in the woman's eyes a moment before she brushed them away. "Okay, you two, back—"

"No, wait. They don't have to go back there. They can stay here with us."

"*Señorita*, I have a lot of work, it'll be—"

"It'll be fine, Rosa. Right, Ring?"

Ring had followed the woman out the door and now looked from Madison to the children and back to Madison again. *She's practically glowing. These kids?* "Whatever you want."

His words seemed to do little to reassure Rosa. "I can't let you—"

Madison waved a hand to halt her words. "Nonsense. They'll be fine. Why don't you two have a seat at the table, and I'll pour you some juice?"

Both kids hustled onto the porch and slid into a chair.

"Are you sure? I don't want them to get in your way."

Maddie put an arm around the woman and turned her toward the house. "We'll be fine. And I'll come get you if we can't handle something. Okay?"

"*¡Gracias!*"

"You're welcome," Maddie responded in answer to the woman's tentative smile. She turned to the table as Rosa left. "Now, what would you like?"

A few minutes later, Sherri appeared with Dave. "Who have we here?"

"This is Tomas and Julieta. They're Rosa's children. These are my friends, Sherri and Dave."

"*Hola,*" the children said between bites.

Dave looked from one child to the other. "And they're here because?"

"They're here because Maddie has a thing for kids, in case you haven't noticed." Sherri poured herself a cup of coffee and pulled out a chair to sit, reaching for a piece of bacon to nibble on. "So, what do you plan on doing with them? They can't eat all day, can they?" Tomas helped himself to more scrambled eggs. "Or maybe they can."

Maddie put some fruit on her plate and sat next to Julieta. "Well, I thought maybe we'd have some breakfast and then I don't know yet."

Ring and Dave sat too. "Dave, maybe you should call the agency and have them send someone out."

"Sure." Dave pulled out his cell phone. "Another housekeeper to replace her?"

Madison set her fork down. "What? No? Rosa's wonderful."

"No, of course not." Ring poured himself a glass of juice. "Someone to watch these two for the day."

"What? I don't need anyone to watch them."

"Madison, I want you to be able to relax. How are you going to do that without some help?"

"I don't need help. There's only two of them, but if I did, there are three other adults here too. Between all of us, we should be able to keep them entertained."

Sherri grinned. "Give it up, Ring. When it comes to kids, Maddie always wins."

# Chapter 12

Rosa and the children had stayed for dinner, then Dave called the car to take them home. Evening settled over the compound as Maddie and Sherri relaxed by a fire on the beach while Ring and Dave mixed drinks in the outdoor kitchen.

"Here—taste this."

Ring eyed the glass Dave held out. "What is it?"

"C'mon, man, just try it."

"Wow. That's potent." He took another sip. "I guess it's not too bad. What's in it?"

"Not too bad? It's great. Pineapple juice, coconut, a couple of other things and lots of rum. Sherri and I concocted it. Two or three of these and you'll be feeling fine." Dave grinned and lifted his head toward the beach. "You know, I didn't want to stay at first, but I'm glad I did. I haven't had this much fun in years. Can you believe we built sand castles today? I haven't done that since I was a kid, but I had a good time. Too bad we lost to the girls. No offense, but it's a good thing you've got acting to fall back on, man, 'cause your building skills suck."

"I missed sand castle competition 101. I was one of those child actors, remember?"

"Yeah, I know. Sorry, Ring."

After the sand castle contest—boys against the girls, Ring and Madison had spent several hours with the kids scouring the beach for sea glass and playing in the surf. "This is the most relaxed I've felt in—" Ring paused. "In I can't remember how long." He took another sip from the glass. "Though I'm not entirely sure if it's the company, or these drinks you keep making."

"Probably some of both, but the company's been great." Dave glanced toward the fire. "They're good people and real. You know what I mean?"

"I do. You and Sherri seem to be hitting it off."

Dave grinned. "She's something else. I wonder if she'd fly out and visit—you know, when we leave here?"

"I don't know. Ask her."

"Yeah, maybe." The man smoothed down his mustache. "Do you think she'd fit in back home?"

Ring shrugged. "Who does?" Sherri's laughter drifted over to them. "She'd fit in after a while, but it'd probably change her."

"Yeah, you're right. That kinda sucks, ya know?" Dave sighed. "I like her 'cause she's different, but if she spends time with me, she won't be. I guess that answers my question."

"Not necessarily."

"What are you talking about? You just said she'd change."

Ring watched the women a moment before saying what'd been on his mind all day. "What if—instead, you changed your lifestyle?"

Dave's heavy eyebrows drew closer together as he frowned. "What are you talking about?"

"Well." Ring paused. "What if you fit yourself into her world?"

"As in moved to East Jockstrap? You're kidding, right? Tell me you're kidding," Dave urged when Ring didn't answer right away. "Ring?"

"It could work."

"No way, man. That's *loco*. There's nothing there. No restaurants, nothing. There's not even a traffic light in that town. It's so dead, the walking dead would just keep on walking."

"I kind of like it. Besides, there's internet and an airport nearby if you needed to go somewhere." Ring spoke more to himself than Dave.

"You'd miss out on too much."

"Like what? Traffic? Smog?"

"No, contacts. You gotta be out there to make contacts, you know, be seen, otherwise they forget about you," Dave insisted.

"Go to parties and awards shows, you mean? Do the talk show circuit? I've had enough of all of that. Besides, it's your job to make contacts. And, if they forget about me, so be it. I've got more money than I can spend now. Which reminds me, I turned down Cam Scott's offer for that part."

"What? When?"

"A couple of days ago."

"How come you didn't tell me? Sixty-five million—that's a lot of money to walk away from. You know it's not good business to turn down too many offers."

"I don't plan on making a habit of it, but shooting begins around the time Madison is supposed to have the baby. Besides, I don't need any more money—"

The racket of crushing ice cut Ring off as Dave punched a button on the blender before turning it off a few moments later. "I'm sorry, I must not have heard you right—did you say you don't need more money?" He splayed a hand on his chest. "Well, personally, I love money and could always use a little more. Plus, have you forgotten? Your ex-wife plans to take a chunk of your change."

"She signed the papers?" *That's one step in the right direction.*

"I wish, but it won't be that easy."

"This divorce has dragged on long enough. I want it over. Make that a priority." Madison's voice caught Ring's attention as she chatted with Sherri. The breeze swirled her loose hair and the firelight bathed her features in a soft warmth no makeup could create. *She has no idea how beautiful she is.* "It's time to move on."

"Sure, boss, but as far as I know Anne still wants half of your future income."

Ring snorted. "That's not going to happen. Put someone on her. It'll probably be for nothing, but you never know. They might turn up something."

"I did hear something interesting about her the other day—there's talk her latest is tanking."

"Really? Hmm." Ring paused. "Tell her I've changed my mind, she can have the house in Malibu after all."

"The beach house? You're kidding?"

"No."

"That's crazy. You paid forty million for that place."

"It doesn't matter, if it settles this. I only bought it because Anne pushed when we first got together. And if it's true about her movie, this offer will be too good for her to pass up."

"Hey, where are those drinks?" Sherri called. "You're supposed to be waiting on us—that was the bet, remember? Maddie may have let you slide, but not me."

"Hold your horses, woman. You're so demanding. I'll be there in a minute." Dave smiled to bely his words before heading toward the house. "It's your money. I'll call the lawyer tomorrow."

Ring studied Madison O'Neill as he neared the fire. She dug bare feet into the sand and rested a hand on the mound of her belly, giving him a warm smile as he settled in the chair next to her. That look caused a sudden pull deep in Ring's gut. *I want her, and it has nothing to do with the baby.*

"Ahh," Sherri sighed. "What a great day. Playing in the sand, a beautiful sunset and now a full moon. This has to be the most gorgeous place on earth. I'd trade sand for snow any day."

Music echoed through the outside speaker system before dropping a bit in volume. A moment later, Dave arrived, carrying the fresh pitcher of drinks. "Here we go." He poured the slushy concoction into each of their glasses. "And for you, madam, the innocent version." He handed Madison a tall glass.

"Fruit juice?"

He nodded.

"Thanks, Dave."

"You're welcome." He held up his glass. "A toast. To a great vacation with great friends, both old and new." He winked at Sherri. "*¡Salud!*"

"Cheers," everyone echoed and took a drink.

Dave turned to Sherri and held out his hand. "Dance?"

Sherri grinned and set her glass down. "Absolutely."

Ring continued to watch Maddie, even as she watched the other couple move to the slow music. "I know it's not the Harvest Ball, but would you like to dance?"

She smiled. "It's just as lovely."

Ring took her into his arms, their movements small in the soft sand. He caught the light floral scent of her perfume. *She smells so good.* After a few moments, Madison relaxed against him with a sigh. He guided her hand to his shoulder, and she looped both arms around his neck. Ring slid his other arm around her back, drawing her closer, the bump of her stomach now pressed against his midsection. A sense of contentment washed over him.

Neither pulled away as another slow song started.

*We belong together. She must feel it too.*

"Ring?" Her voice was a whisper.

"Hmm?"

"What's going on here?" She didn't raise her head as they continued to move to the music.

He laid a kiss along her temple. "Whatever you want."

"I don't know what I want." She stopped and pulled back to look up at him. "But I don't think this can work."

"Yes. It can." He kept his arms around her and brought his head down to meet her lips. "This can so work." He kissed her again, this time more intense as his arms tightened around her.

With a soft groan, she broke off the kiss. "This is crazy. We don't even know each other."

"That's what we're doing here—getting to know each other, remember?"

She remained silent.

He sighed. "Madison, look at me."

She raised her head, confusion clear in her expression.

"I care about you, and I think you feel something for me."

She hesitated a moment. "Yes, maybe I do, but this isn't going to—"

"Shh." He put a finger to her lips. "Shh. We care about each other. That's all we need to know for now." He gave her a squeeze. "How about this? We continue on and see what develops?"

"But what happens when we go back? We come from different worlds."

"We're not going to worry about that right now. Let's enjoy our time here." He kissed her again. "Okay?"

"Okay," she whispered.

# Chapter 13

The next morning, the temperature climbed early. After breakfast, Dave left to take care of some last minute business on the set and Sherri went with him. Ring and Maddie took a walk on the beach and then opted to spend the rest of the morning stretched out side by side on chaise lounges in the shade of the palm trees. They had stayed up late last night and were now content to enjoy the cool ocean breeze sweeping up the beach. They dozed on and off in the quiet of the day. And sometimes they talked. About all kinds of things.

The sun was overhead when Maddie stretched. "I need to get up." But she didn't move.

"Why?" Ring's eyes remained closed.

"Because I need to start lunch."

He lifted his head to look at her. "Didn't we hire people to do that?"

"Yes, *you* did, but it's Manuela's day off and Rosa's mother is very sick, so I told her to stay home today."

"Okay. Dave can call the agency and—"

"No."

"Fine. He can stop and pick up—"

"No, don't do anything." Madison sat up. "Ring, you might not understand this, but I like doing things for myself."

"But you don't have to—"

"Yes, I do. In my world, I do. I garden. I cook. I clean. And I like doing it...well, not the cleaning part so much, but I still do it."

"But you don't have to, Madison." He sat up too and faced her as he reached for her hands. "I've been thinking. I think we should get together."

"What? Get together? Have you forgotten you're still married?"

"Not likely, but I'm working on it." He paused a moment. "Maddie, we're good together."

"Good together? Maybe here in Shangri-la." She stood. "It's beautiful, but it's not the real world—for either of us."

"It could be."

Maddie shook her head. "No, it can't be. Your life is premieres, parties and people fulfilling your every whim. Mine is children with runny noses, a drafty house and sometimes small town minds, but it's my small town. I don't want to change that."

"Madison, listen for a—"

"No, Ring. I've made the gossip chain in Northam and that's bad enough, but every move you make is dissected by the media. The whole world sees your mistakes. I couldn't handle that."

"It's not that bad."

"Yes, it is," she said with an exasperated sigh. "I'm going in and start lunch." She left for the kitchen.

Ring followed. "Madison, I think you're worrying about this too much."

"Maybe. But I don't plan on finding out." She tied on an apron and pulled marinated chicken and chopped vegetables from the fridge.

He was silent for several minutes as he watched her prepare the meal. "Fine. We can talk about this later." He ignored her frown. "What can I help with?"

"There's not much to do. The salad is all made, and the stir fry is just about done." She gave the contents of the pan another stir with a wooden spatula. "But I could use a glass of ice water, if you don't mind." She opened a drawer and pulled out a kettle. "And then, if you could put some water in this to cook rice, that'd be great."

The only sounds in the kitchen were the sizzle of food and running water.

"Here you go." He sat her glass of water down on the counter and picked up the kettle.

"Thank you." She took a sip, but kept her eyes on the *sauté* pan.

Fifteen minutes passed before the front door opened and closed and voices could be heard in the living room.

"That must be Sherri and Dave. Perfect timing. The rice is done." Maddie put the lid back on the pot.

Dave hurried into the kitchen, a frown on his face. "You're not going to like this." His tone was low. "I want you to know, it wasn't my idea."

"What're you talking about?" Ring set out dishes. "Where's Sherri? Madison made lunch."

"She's in her room. We stopped off for a drink. I didn't know he was there."

"Who?" Ring stepped around the counter.

"Booth Rainshaw."

"What? You didn't bring him back here?"

"He said he hadn't partied with you in a long time. He wanted to stop by."

Ring paced the open length of the kitchen as he scraped a hand through his hair several times. "You know damn well there's a reason why I haven't seen him."

"I know. I know." Dave gave a helpless shrug. "What was I supposed to do? You're doing a movie with the guy in a few months!"

Maddie stopped stirring. "Are you talking about the British actor?"

"Yes." Ring moved closer. "Look, Madison. I didn't plan this, but Booth—"

"Hey, Ring, old man! Long time no see." Booth Rainshaw strode into the kitchen. Rail thin, his bleached hair, though short, stood out in all directions. Dark circles under his eyes were further emphasized by smudged eye liner. "How've ya been, mate?"

"Good."

"Where's Anne? Is she here? I thought she'd be here. Last time I partied with her, she said something about you guys getting together again."

Ring could feel Madison's stare. "She isn't here."

"Huh? That's too bad. That woman knows how to party." Booth took a pull off his cigarette and studied Ring through a haze of smoke. "You look good though, man. You been workin' out? I plan on starting when I get home from this shit hole." He rubbed his hands up and down his arms. "But right now, I need a little something." He reached into his shirt pocket and pulled out a small black case. He unzipped it and set it on the counter. "Buggar me. I must've left my mirror in the restaurant bathroom. Got one I can borrow?"

Ring shook his head. "No." He glanced at Madison. Her eyes were locked on the tiny plastic bags that littered the counter top.

"No problem. One of these will do." The man picked up a china plate off the table.

"No." Ring took the plate from his hand and put it in the sink. "Look, I'm sorry, Booth, but we were about to have lunch."

"Lunch? Oh yeah. That's why we were at the restaurant, but we ran into Dave here before we could order." Booth inhaled deeply. "Something does smell good in here. Man, I've been buzzing for a few days, but suddenly I'm starved." He took another drag off his cigarette, creating a long ash that dropped onto the counter as he moved closer. "Shit." He looked around for a moment, shrugged and then dropped the remainder of the cigarette into Maddie's glass of ice water. "Is it ready?"

She looked at Ring, but said nothing.

Booth pantomimed the motion of eating and then pointed at the pan. "Is it ready? *¿Habla usted Inglés?* Does she speak English?" He glanced at Ring and then back to Maddie, his gaze landing on her midsection. "Well, there's at least one language she understands." He guffawed at his own joke.

"She's not the—"

"*Lo siento, señor, no Inglés.*" Madison arranged her features into a smile, but shook her head and held up one hand, fingers spread apart. "*Cinco minutos.*"

"Five minutes? Great!" Booth rubbed his hands together and stepped to the doorway. "Hey, guys, chow's on."

Maddie laid out a bed of rice and heaped the stir fry on top before setting the platter in the middle of the table.

"This looks good." Booth dropped into a chair and a second later, a man and woman appeared and slid into chairs on either side of him. Both were dressed in black, emphasizing their pale skin, each as thin as their friend. Booth heaped his plate and shoveled a mouthful in. "This is great," he said around the food.

Maddie nodded and turned away.

"Hey, where are you goin'? Stick around." Booth grinned. "You might get lucky after dinner." He chewed a moment in contemplation. "I don't think I've ever done it with a pregnant maid before."

"Prague." The man beside him said between bites.

"Really?" Booth shook his head. "I can't remember; was she any good?"

Maddie made a hasty exit.

"Hey, where you going, girlie?" Booth called after her. "Isn't she serving us? Where are our drinks?"

"Don't talk to—"

"What would you like to drink, Booth?" Dave cut Ring off as he put himself between his friend and the other man.

"Hmm, how about bourbon? You got any bourbon? Might as well get this party started."

Madison rolled over at the knock on her door. "Who is it?" She'd listened to loud conversation, laughter and music for the last two hours.

"It's me, Ring."

"Come in."

Ring closed the door behind him and came to sit on the edge of the bed. "Are you okay?"

She nodded.

"I'm sorry. I didn't know they were coming."

"I know that. I hope you don't have many friends like that—he's a disgusting man."

"First of all, he's not my friend. He's someone I've worked with in the past, and Dave and I got rid of them as fast as we could. Booth Rainshaw's part of a life I left behind, but if I was anywhere near as obnoxious as he is while I was using, somebody should have put me out of my misery."

"You don't remember? Seriously?"

He shook his head. "No, just bits and pieces."

"Well, if you ever need any parts filled in, ask Sherri. She'll tell you all about your exploits. She's tried to tell me often enough."

"What? How does she know?"

"Those tabloids newspapers. She reads them all the time."

He sighed. "You can't believe those things. I'm sure if I'd done half of what they've printed I'd be dead by now."

"Like what?"

"I don't know. I've never read them."

"Okay. Ahh, let's see. Did you steal a police car?"

"No."

"Do you own fourteen estates?"

He shook his head. "Nope. I'm not sure, but I think it's only seven—maybe eight."

"You have eight properties?"

He shrugged. "I haven't decided which one I want to call home yet."

She shook her head. "Okay, were you abducted by aliens?"

He frowned. "Really?"

"Sorry." Madison sat up and leaned against the pillows. "What made you stop?"

"Using?"

Maddie nodded, her expression serious.

"Well, I wanted to, but I couldn't for a long time—not even when it was my father's haggard face staring back at me in the mirror every morning." He rubbed a hand along the back of his neck. "Then there was this one night. Anne was having one of her famous parties at the Malibu house, and I ended up passing out on the beach. When I came to, I was in the water. I was so high, it took several tries before I realized I was caught in a rip tide. Panic set in for a few minutes, but after that, I was exhausted and no closer to the beach. Then as I drifted to catch my breath, it seems like everything got real quiet and this calm came over me. That's when I knew I wanted to live. I swore if I got out alive, I was going to clean up my act. After what seemed like hours, I finally made it out." Ring shook his head. "When I got back to the house, no one had even missed me. I checked into rehab the next day. I've been clean ever since. No drugs."

"I know it couldn't have been easy for you."

"Maybe it wouldn't have been so hard if I could have seen myself as I saw Booth today. But you're right, even now it isn't easy. I've tried to stay away from anyone who uses, but there have been a few situations like this one. And every time I'm around it, a small part of me wants to do a few lines...according to the rehab docs the urge will always be there." He sighed. "They claim it'll get easier as time passes, but I don't know..."

The sadness in his dark eyes drew Madison in. She slipped her arms around him. "Then believe it will—and it will."

"Thank you. With you, I can almost believe it." He sighed and pulled her closer. "Please don't ever do that again."

She pulled back. "Do what?"

"Pretend to be the maid. You're beautiful and intelligent. Any man would be lucky to have you in his life—including me."

"What else could I do? How did you plan on explaining me to your wife's friends?"

"I didn't plan on explaining anything—it's none of their business."

"This is all getting complicated."

"It's not. It's simple." He slipped his hand into hers. "I'm sorry they ate our lunch. Dave and Sherri went out to pick up some dinner. How about a short walk while we wait? I know I could use some fresh air."

Ring continued to hold her hand throughout their stroll, not letting go as they climbed the steps to the back porch of Maddie's house. A delicious smell wafted from the kitchen as they stepped through the doorway.

Maddie's stomach grumbled in hunger. "Sherri, whatever you got, it smells delicious."

"Mmm. It does. We stopped at this little restaurant Dave's been to a couple of times and got several different things to try. I'll finish putting it out if you guys want to set the table."

"I'll make drinks," Dave volunteered.

The noise from the large screen television in the adjoining family room mixed with laughter and conversation as everyone relaxed and enjoyed the delicious food. When finished, everyone moved to the sofa to figure out their plans for the evening.

"I'm stuffed." Dave patted his stomach. "I vote we stay right here."

Sherri eyed him. "And do what?"

"Take a nap?" He raised his brows in hope.

"No way." Sherri shook her head. "I vote a fire and more dancing on—"

"Hey, hey." Dave interrupted as he waved his hand. "Shh. Look, man, that's you on TV." He tossed the remote on the table after turning up the volume. A photo of Ring in a tux flashed on the screen.

Sherri whistled and nodded. "Lookin' sharp, Mr. Stanford."

"I remember that." Dave pointed in the direction of the screen. "The SAG awards. Last year? Or was it the year before?"

Ring shrugged.

*"In entertainment news, the new Ring Stanford movie has finally wrapped and insiders say all the cost overruns will pay off in the end; it's a shoo-in for Oscar gold."*

Dave slapped Ring on the back. "Did you hear that, man? Oscar! Damn...I knew it. This calls for another drink." He crossed to the blender to pour more of the frozen concoction.

Madison glanced at Ring. His look of discomfort changed as his gaze narrowed in the direction of the television. A picture of a beautiful, dark haired woman in a low-cut red gown filled the screen. Maddie recognized her.

*"In related news, it seems Mr. Stanford's estranged wife, Anne Reese Miller hasn't been as lucky. Early reports are box office sales for Encroachment, her latest film, have been dismal despite her collaboration with famed director, Arthur Von Timber. Word is, their off-screen collaboration is over too. What's next for this Hollywood beauty? Believe it or not, the rumor is she'll be co-starring with Ring Stanford in an upcoming project later this year. We'll have to keep an eye on that story. This is Barrett—"*

The television screen went black.

Ring held the remote in his hand as he looked at Dave. "What the hell was that about?"

"I have no idea." Dave shook his head. "I told you a long time ago she was *loco*. You shouldn't have married—"

The high-pitched buzz of cell phones echoed in the quiet room. Ring's sat on the coffee table. Dave pulled his from his pocket and glanced at the number. "We should take these."

"No." Ring made no move to pick up his phone, its minute vibration moving it along the polished wood. It stopped moving just short of falling onto the floor.

Dave's phone continued to buzz. "Ring, we've got to respond. At least get out a press release."

"And say what, Dave? She's lying?" Ring placed a hand on the back of his neck. "Something's going on. I don't know what she's up to, but you know damn well Anne started that rumor." He tipped his head to flex tight muscles as his phone buzzed again. "Let's get out of here." He looked in Madison's direction. "Didn't you mention you wanted to shop for souvenirs?"

"Yes, but we don't have to do it tonight."

"Ring, it might not be such a good idea to go—"

"It'll be fine, Dave." Ring's phone stopped ringing. "We can go to some of the shops away from the main plaza. Call the car. I'm going to change." He headed off to the other house.

Sherri set her drink on the counter, her smile gone. "Dave, what's going on?"

His phone rang again. Dave looked at it for a moment before finally shoving it back in his pocket. "That woman—his wife is crazy." He shook his head. "I mean like scary crazy." He headed toward the glass door. "You ladies might want to get dressed. Mr. Stanford wants to go out."

# Chapter 14

No one spoke on the short drive downtown. Ring instructed the driver to let them out along a side street.

"I'm calling the security detail." Dave eyed the throngs of people crowding the streets. "They can be here in ten minutes."

"We'll be fine. No one even knows we're still here." Ring walked at the front with his head down, his strides long. Loud music blasted out the open windows of a bar up ahead. Maddie watched several people stare as Ring passed, despite his baseball cap and sunglasses. With Dave and Sherri ahead of her, Madison did her best to keep up, but lagged behind in the congestion on the sidewalk. *Where are they?* She attempted to work her way through the crowd loitering outside the bar. Someone pushed her from behind. Maddie stumbled and in turn pushed someone else.

"What the hell?" The man turned, the front of his light blue shirt wet. "You spilled my drink."

"I'm sorry." Maddie opened her purse as people continued to jostle her. "Here. Please take this and buy another drink."

"What about my shirt, huh?"

"Madison, are you all right?" Ring shouldered his way to her side and spotted the twenty dollar bill in her hand. "What's going on?" He took a step closer.

"Nothing, man. She spilled my drink. No big deal."

Ring pulled off his sunglasses and ignored the man, instead focusing on Maddie. "Are you okay?"

"Yes, I just need to get out of this crowd."

He nodded. "I'm sorry. I was wrapped up in my own thoughts. Let's—"

"Hey, I know you, you're Ring Stanford. Hey, you guys, look who it is—Ring Stanford." Several sets of eyes turned their way. "I like your movies. Can I get your autograph?" The man was all smiles now.

Someone's warm breath touched the back of Maddie's neck, along with several bodies pressing closer as more people crowded in around them. Numerous scraps of paper and cocktail napkins dangled from arms extended past Maddie in Ring's direction.

Ring slipped his glasses back on and put his hands up, palms out. "I'm sorry. I don't have a pen on me." In an instant, several pens were thrust past Maddie's head, one almost poking her in the eye. "Can you handle this for a couple of minutes?" He kept his voice low. "If not, it's okay, we can go."

"I'll be okay."

He signed his name numerous times and still more people crowded around them. Breasts pressed against her back before someone shoved Maddie to the side in an attempt to get closer to Ring. She caught a glimpse of pink and very blonde hair before Ring's arm encircled her. He tucked her close to his body as he backed up. "Dave?"

"Right here." Dave Martinez stepped up to address the crowd. "That's all the autographs, folks, but I've got some free passes to Ring's next movie."

Ring kept his arm around Maddie as they joined Sherri up the street a few moments later. "We're going through here. Dave will catch up." He led them down a short side street that opened into a smaller mall. There weren't nearly as many people here and no bars. Several gift shops lined each side of the area. "Dave's right, we should've brought security. I'm sorry. I wasn't thinking." He turned Maddie toward him. "Are you okay?"

She swallowed. "Yes, I'm fine. That was scary."

"You get used to it."

"I could never get used to that," she uttered in a shaky voice.

He studied her a moment. "I won't let anything happen to you. I promise. I can have Dave call the detail when he gets here if it makes you feel better. In the meantime, why don't you ladies take a look around in some of these shops? No one will bother you."

*A bunch of big guys in dark suits? Like that won't draw any attention.* Madison pushed a stray strand of hair out of her face. "I'm sure we'll be fine."

He nodded. "It's probably a good idea if I wait out here. Dave should be along in a minute."

"Maddie, are you really okay? Do you need to sit down?" Concern laced Sherri's questions.

Madison dragged in a deep breath through her nose and exhaled. "I'm better now. I'd like to get our souvenirs while we have the chance." She gave Sherri a tremulous smile. "C'mon, let's look around."

The women checked out several small stores stuffed with everything from sombreros to pottery. After the fourth shopkeeper offered them a discount because it was his birthday, Madison couldn't help but laugh.

Dave and Ring stood in the street in deep conversation. Maddie glanced out just as a group of several women came up to Ring. He obliged as they asked for autographs and pictures. One of them, a busty blond, in a bright pink top, pressed close and planted a kiss on his lips as her friends snapped picture after picture. *Okay, enough is enough.* "Sherri, I saw something a little further down the street I wanted to take a look at. I'll be right back." With that, Madison slipped out the door and hurried away.

"Madison."

She didn't stop at Ring's call. *Those women have cameras. I've got to get away.* She took the next left and hurried down the street, finally stopping to ease a stitch in her side. She leaned against a stucco wall, head down and hands resting on her thighs as she tried to catch her breath in the humid air. Voices across the street caught her attention. In the gathering dusk, Madison spotted several men staring from a ramshackle porch. They laughed and beckoned her forth, one holding up two bottles of liquor. "*Hola, señorita.* Come join the party."

She looked around for the nearest shop. There weren't any, just more dilapidated buildings, most of them dark inside. *I'd better get back to the car.* She shoved off the wall as two of the men from the porch headed toward her.

"Where you goin'?"

*Move. Move.*

They fell into step with her, one on each side. "Hey, pretty lady, what's your rush? You want a drink?" The man's long black hair partially covered several tattoos marking his shirtless chest and arms. He shoved a bottle in front of her face.

Maddie knocked his hand away and kept walking.

The other man snorted. *"Ella piensa que es demasiado buena."*

*Oh God, what'd I get myself into?*

"Is that true, bitch? Do you think you're too good for us?" The tattooed man grabbed Madison's arm and swung her around to thump against the wall. Her breath escaped in a whoosh. He laid a meaty forearm across her chest and leaned in, his alcohol laced breath washing over her face as his stringy hair brushed the front of her dress. "That true, huh? You too good? That hump under your dress says otherwise."

Madison shook her head. His added weight made it hard to draw breath. "No." It was barely a whisper.

"I didn't think so." He put the bottle to her lips. "Have a drink."

She cringed against the wall and shook her head.

He shifted and slid his arm up until it rested across her windpipe. "Drink."

She shook her head again.

He leaned more weight against his arm until Madison struggled for breath.

"Drink."

She nodded and clawed at his arm at the same time.

He put the bottle to her mouth and tipped it up. Tequila burned a path across her tongue. Unable to breathe, Madison choked, most of the alcohol running down her chin, under his arm and into the V-neckline of her sun dress.

"*Puta*, you're wasting it! But don't worry, I'll take care of it."
He bent to lick the liquid off her chest.

Over the top of his head Maddie glimpsed the other man
laughing, most of his teeth gone. Nausea welled as the tattooed
man dipped his tongue in the space between her breasts. Dizzy
from lack of oxygen, her knees buckled. Only the man's dirty arm
held her upright.

"Get away from her, or I'll kill you."

Madison tried to focus on the voice. *Ring?*

The man holding Madison raised his head. "Get the fuck outta
here." He turned to his companion. "*Deshazte de ellos si quieres un
turno.*"

A second later there was the distinct click of metal against
metal. "*No es una decisión inteligente, amigo.*"

*Dave? Does he have a gun?* Maddie drew a breath as the man's
arm left her throat. Shattering glass and the splatter of liquid
accompanied him yanking her in front of him. He squeezed her
around the midsection, the broken tequila bottle pressed to the side
of her protruding abdomen.

The toothless man put his hands up and shook his head. "*No
quiero ningún problema. Fue su idea.*"

"*Bastardo*, coward," the man hissed near her ear. "You want
the *puta*?" He shouted as he backed up, taking her with him.

It was dark, but Maddie could make out the two forms in front
of her, and there was no mistaking Ring's voice. "Let her go."

"I don't think so. If I do, your friend will put a bullet in me."

"If you don't, you'll wish my friend had put a bullet in you."

The tone of Ring's words made Maddie shiver.

"Shit. I'm gettin' outta here, and you're comin' with me."

A shake of her head brought more pressure on the broken bottle. "Okay."

The man shuffled backwards at an angle, his grip so tight, she was back to struggling for breath. Out of the corner of her eye, Maddie could see they were in the mouth of an alleyway. *They're never going to find me after this.*

A burst of stucco over their heads halted the man's progress.

"What are you guys, fuckin' *loco*? You coulda' shot me!"

"I'm going to—"

The sudden shrill sound of a whistle and running feet interrupted Ring. Half a dozen uniformed men came around the corner with flashlights and pistols drawn. There were shouts of "*Policía!*" Dave dropped his gun and put his hands up. The beams from numerous lights illuminated Maddie and her captor. "¡*Suelta el arma*! Drop your weapon!"

"I ain't goin' back to jail. Maybe another time, bitch!" The man gave Maddie a shove. She hit the ground hard and tried to catch her breath as several sets of feet pounded by her.

"Maddie." Ring gently lifted her to a sitting position and pulled her into his arms. "You're safe. You're safe." He stroked her hair. "Don't move. It's going to be okay."

Madison rested against his chest, dragging in deep breaths as she took stock of her condition.

"I'm so sorry. This has been a bad night."

"Not your fault. It's mine." Her words were a whisper. "I shouldn't have left by myself."

"Why did you? What happened?"

*What am I supposed to say? I didn't like it when that woman kissed him?* "I guess I wasn't thinking."

He placed a finger under her chin and lifted her face. "Are you hurt?"

"I feel pretty roughed up, but other than a few bruises, I think I'm okay."

"Good. Do you want to try and stand?"

She nodded. "Let me get in a better position, and then could you give me a little help?" Maddie rolled to her knees and held her hands out. Ring tugged her to her feet.

"Aww, that hurts."

"What hurts?"

"My arm." Maddie touched the skin and her fingers came away wet. "I must have scraped it when I fell."

"Let's get you into the light." They stepped over to one of the policeman. Maddie gasped when the flashlight beam washed over her. Two slashes ran at an angle across her forearm. Her movements had increased the blood flow; it was now dripping off her fingertips.

"The bottle. It must have cut me."

"Let me look, please." Another policeman stepped forward to examine the wounds. "Pedro, get the first aid kit." A moment later he doused the wounds with peroxide and covered them with gauze before winding more gauze around Madison's forearm. "That will help, but you must get to the hospital. It is deep; you need more care than I can give. One of my men can drive you."

"I'm going with you."

"A statement, *señor*—I'm sorry, what's your name?"

"Ring Stanford."

"*Señor* Stanford, I need to take—" The officer stopped mid-sentence and shone his flashlight in Ring's face. "Ring Stanford, the actor? Didn't you just do a movie here?"

"Yes." Ring kept his gaze on the policeman despite the harsh glare of the light. "I'm going with her to the hospital."

Maddie put a hand on his arm. "You don't have to. I'll be fine."

"*Señor* Stanford, your wife will be in good hands."

"I'm not—"

"I'm going with her."

"Sir, a firearm was discharged by your friend. Reports should be filled out."

"Should be?" Ring studied the policeman a moment before turning to Maddie. "Why don't you wait in the car? I'll be there in a minute."

"But, Ring, you don't—"

"It's okay. I'll be right there."

"Pedro, take Mrs. Stanford to the car."

Madison acquiesced and a young policeman escorted her to a car before climbing behind the steering wheel. Ten minutes later, Ring joined her and they pulled away. "Where's Dave?"

"He's tying up some loose ends, and then he and Sherri are going back to the house to wait for my call."

"Sherri! Oh, my gosh—I forgot about Sherri. Is she okay?"

"She's fine. She's the one that got the police."

"Thank goodness." Madison shoved a hand through her disheveled hair. "What a day."

"How's your arm?"

"It's starting to throb."

"We should be there soon."

The Emergency Department was noisy as Ring and Maddie listened to the doctor in the tiny curtained off area.

"*Señora*, the good news is there doesn't appear to be any serious nerve or tendon damage. So, your options—you could have general anesthesia to have the wounds closed; it would be relatively painless without too much risk to the pregnancy."

"Without too much risk? What does that mean?"

The doctor shrugged. "Every surgery carries some risk."

"What's my other option?"

"Well, you can have a local anesthetic, and it can be sutured. But I must warn you, there are several spots where the lacerations are quite deep. It'll take a lot of local anesthetic to repair it, and even then I won't be able to guarantee your comfort."

"There's no risk to the baby though, doing it that way?"

The doctor shook his head.

"Then that's the way I want it done."

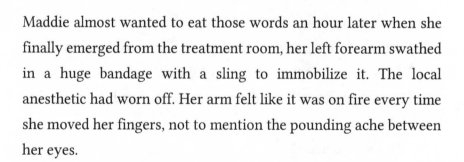

Maddie almost wanted to eat those words an hour later when she finally emerged from the treatment room, her left forearm swathed in a huge bandage with a sling to immobilize it. The local anesthetic had worn off. Her arm felt like it was on fire every time she moved her fingers, not to mention the pounding ache between her eyes.

Ring parked her wheelchair outside the entryway. He'd stayed with her throughout the procedure, holding her uninjured hand. "Are you sure you're okay? You're really pale."

Maddie gave him a wan smile. "I have a headache."

"I'll ask the nurse for something to help. I'll be right back." A few minutes later he returned to the waiting area with a small paper cup. Through the large glass windows, Maddie watched him stuff a bill into a vending machine. Scooping up the bottle of water, Ring was approached by the young policeman who'd driven them to the hospital. *What's he still doing here?* Ring spoke to him for a moment and then headed in her direction. Another man entered the area carrying a black case and went to the vending machine before chatting with the policeman.

"Here you go." Ring handed her the small cup and then cracked open the bottle of water. She took a sip to get the pills down and handed it back to him.

"Why don't you try a few more sips?"

She drank a little more.

Ring sat on the bench facing her. "I called Dave. They should be here in a few minutes."

"Good. I need to get out of these clothes and clean up. I must look like a wreck."

He shook his head and scooted forward on the bench. "You look tired, but who wouldn't be after what you've been through tonight. I'm really sorry."

"How do you stand it all the time? People crowded around you like that? It's been a scary night."

He shrugged. "It comes with the territory. And you, scared?" He reached out to touch her cheek. "After what I just saw you sit through, I think you have more courage than anyone I've ever met."

"That's not—" A gasp escaped her lips.

"What's wrong?" Ring moved closer.

Maddie sighed and put a hand on her stomach. "Thank goodness. The baby just gave me a good kick. Finally. It hasn't moved that much in the last few hours."

"Are you sure everything's okay?" Concern etched his features.

"I think so. Here, feel." She returned Ring's smile as the baby's next kick landed against his palm. He kept his hand there and leaned in. His dark eyes held her in place.

"I thought I'd lost you tonight."

His lips touched hers. The kiss was soft, but deepened. He laid his hands on either side of her face, giving her several more kisses, each as gentle as the last. After a few moments, he slid back on the bench at the approach of headlights.

The long dark car stopped, and Dave and Sherri got out.

"Maddie, are you okay? I was so worried." Sherri bent down and wrapped her arms around Madison's neck. "What the heck did they do to your arm?"

"Put it back together." Maddie patted her friend's back and glanced past Ring as a quick movement caught her eye. The man she'd seen with the case earlier stood at the windows watching them.

"S.O.B." Dave muttered when he spotted the man. He bent down next to Ring and whispered something in his ear. Ring stood up as if the bench was electrified. "Okay, let's get you home." He guided Maddie into the car and climbed in after her. Dave and Sherri followed.

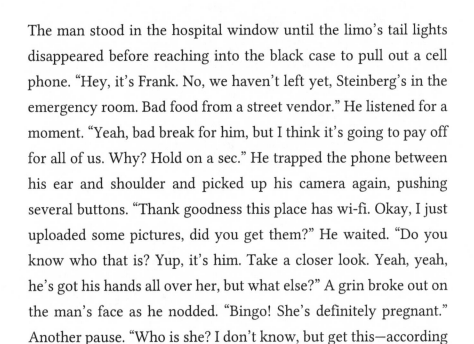

The man stood in the hospital window until the limo's tail lights disappeared before reaching into the black case to pull out a cell phone. "Hey, it's Frank. No, we haven't left yet, Steinberg's in the emergency room. Bad food from a street vendor." He listened for a moment. "Yeah, bad break for him, but I think it's going to pay off for all of us. Why? Hold on a sec." He trapped the phone between his ear and shoulder and picked up his camera again, pushing several buttons. "Thank goodness this place has wi-fi. Okay, I just uploaded some pictures, did you get them?" He waited. "Do you know who that is? Yup, it's him. Take a closer look. Yeah, yeah, he's got his hands all over her, but what else?" A grin broke out on the man's face as he nodded. "Bingo! She's definitely pregnant." Another pause. "Who is she? I don't know, but get this—according to the cop who drove her here, she's Mrs. Ring Stanford." He held the phone away from his ear a moment. "No, no, I'm pretty sure he's still married to Anne Reese Miller. Now, that bitch is a piece of work. Who can blame him? I almost feel bad we're going to wreck his fun." He snickered. "I said almost. Business is business."

# Chapter 15

Maddie finished the laborious task of tugging the sun dress over her head with one hand and slid the straps onto her shoulders. She sat down on the edge of the bed again and worked her heavily bandaged arm back into the sling before glancing at the alarm clock. Ten o'clock. It'd taken her almost an hour to wash up and get dressed. She pushed her hair out of her face. *I'm going to have to get Sherri to do my hair. I wonder if Ring and Dave will come over for breakfast.*

A heavy door slammed somewhere outside, followed a few minutes later by another. *What's going on?* Barefoot, Madison padded across the room and pulled open the bedroom door. The living room was dark; someone had pulled the blinds. She headed toward the kitchen. It was dark and deserted. *What's going on? Where is everyone?* She heard low voices coming from the back porch. She stepped through the glass door and stopped short. Bamboo blinds filled the archways of the porch, casting the outdoor space in dimness. Ring, Dave and Sherri sat at the table drinking coffee. "What's going on?"

Ring jumped up. "Maddie, what are you doing up? Don't you think you should rest a little while longer?"

Maddie shook her head. "No. Why is the house so dark?"

"How about some orange juice?" Sherri rose and came around the table to pull out a chair. "Have a seat. Dave, would you get Maddie some juice?" Dave left as Madison sat down at the table.

"How about I fix your hair? Hold on a second, I'll get a brush." Sherri hurried away.

Madison looked up at Ring. "What's going on?"

He dropped back into the chair and studied his hands a moment before finally lifting his gaze to meet hers. "Look, Maddie, there's—"

"Here we go." Sherri gave her a pat on the shoulder. "I'll have you fixed up in a minute." She went to work on Madison's hair. "You'll be feeling like your old self in no time." She tugged on a snarl. "Sorry. Dave, where's that orange juice?"

*What's going on?*

"Here you go, Madison." Dave set the juice in front of her. "Drink up. You'll need your strength." He sat down on the other side of the table.

"For what? What's going on? Why are all the blinds closed?"

No one answered for a moment. Sherri finished her braid. "Maddie, sweetie, don't worry about—"

"The press found out."

Madison turned her attention to Ring. "What?"

He sighed. "There were pictures taken of us last night."

"What? When?" Maddie sputtered. "That can't be. I was—we were careful."

Ring reached into the chair next to him and laid several newspapers on the table in front of Maddie. She pulled one closer. LOVE CHILD, the headline blared. Underneath it, two pictures of her and Ring kissing. "Outside the hospital?"

He nodded.

She pushed the papers away. "This can't be happening."

Ring reached over and gave her hand a squeeze. "I'm so sorry. But we'll deal with it. Don't worry."

"Don't worry? You're kidding, right?" She stood, shoving the chair back in the process. "That may be easy for you, but not for me. I didn't want this!"

Ring still had her hand. He gave it a gentle tug. "Maddie, sit down. Please don't get worked up. It's not good for the—"

Maddie yanked her hand back. "I didn't want this." She turned and left the room. Another loud bang outside stopped her at the front door. She reached for the knob.

"Don't open the door."

She ignored Ring's warning and wrenched the door open.

"Look, look. It's her. Madison O'Neill, right? Ms. O'Neill, would you like to make a statement?"

"What happened to your arm?"

"Can you tell us how you and Ring Stanford met?"

"You're carrying his baby, right?"

"He's still married. Did you know that? Does his wife know about the baby?"

"Is it a boy or a girl?"

"Is he in there? Would he care to make a statement?"

Camera clicks and whirs accompanied the barrage of questions shouted from the rooftops of several vans parked on the other side of the compound wall.

Maddie stood frozen, unsure of what to do. Someone pulled her back and closed the door. She sagged against the wood of the heavy portal.

"Don't worry. We'll figure this out." Ring put an arm around her. "Madison, in a few days they'll go on to someone else and forget all about us."

"Forget about us? In your world maybe, but not in mine. Every person I know will never forget this or let me forget it." A sob caught in her throat. "I can't go back home now. Where am I supposed to go?"

"Maddie, please don't get worked up about this, I'm going back to Northam with you. I'll take care—"

"You've done enough." She broke free of his embrace. "Just leave me alone." She made it to her room and turned the lock before bursting into tears.

"Madison, please come out, we need to talk about this."

She didn't respond to Ring's quiet words. Throughout the day and into the evening, he and Sherri knocked on her door several times and tried to persuade her to come out. Maddie didn't open the door.

After midnight the house became quiet.

At one o'clock, Madison picked up the phone and dialed the number on the card she held. "Hello, it's Madison O'Neill. Do you remember me? Good. Listen, I need a ride to the airport. An hour? That'll work. No, not here. I'll meet you a quarter of a mile east of the compound. Just pull to the side of the road and wait. Yes, I'm sure. Thank you, Carlos. I'll see you then."

Twenty minutes later, she set two envelopes on the night stand and picked up her purse. Madison O'Neill slipped through the glass door in her bedroom to the small porch and moved along the water's edge to disappear into the night.

# Chapter 16

*Thank goodness.* Relief washed over Madison as she scanned the gate area.

Brian Holt stepped forward and gave her a hard hug. "Maddie, what's going on? Are you okay? What happened to your arm?"

"I'm okay." She patted his shirt front before pulling out of his arms. "Let's get out of here. Please." She headed toward the glass doors of the exit.

"Where's your coat? What about your luggage?"

"I don't have any."

"Maddie, stop."

She turned. Brian hadn't moved. "What?"

"You're kidding, right? What happened? Where's Sherri?"

Several heads turned at his raised voice. Maddie hurried to grab his arm. "Come on. Let's go."

"No. Not until you tell me what's going on." Brian stood rooted to the spot.

*Oh—of all times for him to be stubborn!* "Can we get out of this terminal, please?"

"Why? What's the matter?"

Madison glanced around. A woman seated in the waiting area pulled a cell phone out of her pocket. Maddie ducked behind Brian.

"What're you doing?" he asked without moving.

"That lady's taking a picture of me."

"What lady?"

"Over there."

"Where?"

Maddie took a peek. The woman was gone. She stepped out from behind Brian. "Well, I thought she was."

Brian shook his head.

"What? I thought she was." Madison sighed. "Look, Bri, I'm really tired. I haven't slept in two days. I had to change planes twice to get here, I'm starving and," she adjusted the strap on her sling, "I need to take something for this."

"Fine." Brian whipped off his coat and dropped it on to her shoulders. "The truck's right outside." They headed out the exit. "Where do you want to eat? Burlington has lots of decent restaurants."

"No, I don't want to go in anywhere. Can we grab some take out?"

He helped her into the truck before climbing in on the driver's side. "Sure, I guess." Brian started the engine, but didn't put it in gear, just sat staring out the windshield. "I'm not moving until you answer some questions." His voice was quiet.

Maddie threw her good arm up in the air. "Fine."

"What happened?"

"Oh, Bri, things got a little crazy, that's all."

"Is my sister all right?"

"Yes, of course she is."

"Why isn't she with you?"

"I didn't tell her I was leaving—I didn't tell anyone, but I left her a note."

"What happened to your arm?"

"I got cut by a broken bottle."

Neither of them said anything for a few moments.

"I read some stuff in one of those papers Sherri buys...is it true? Is it his baby?" Brian kept his gaze on the distant landscape.

Maddie didn't respond.

"How can that be?"

She sighed. "Dr. Carson."

"Who?"

"Dr. Carson. The specialist I went to in Boston."

"He introduced you two?"

"Not exactly. Look, Brian, it's a long story."

"Well, it'll take us two hours to get back to Northam—that should be plenty of time."

"I'm not going back. I'm not ready to face anyone yet."

Her statement brought Brian's head around. "What? Of course you're going back. It's your home. I'm sure if you ignore those reporters and TV people, they'll go away eventually."

"I was talking about Willa Mae—what reporters? What are you talking about?"

"Nothing." Brian put the truck in gear and a moment later turned onto the street. "What do you want to eat? Is a burger and fries okay?"

"What reporters?"

"Damn it!" Brian slammed the heel of his hand against the steering wheel a couple of times. "It's nothing. Never mind. A burger, yes?"

"Brian Holt, you tell me what's going on, right now."

He shook his head and let out an exasperated sigh. "All right, all right! They started showing up yesterday morning. By last night there were a boat load of them all over town, taking all kinds of pictures and asking everyone questions."

Maddie swallowed. "What are people saying?"

"I have no idea. Nothing around me." Brian turned into a drive-through to place his food order and pulled ahead to the next window. "There were even a bunch of them camped on your front lawn. I tried to get them to move, but it took getting Noah Lawson over there to remove them, and that was only after he threatened them with a gun."

"What?"

"Don't worry. I don't think he really would've shot them." Brian turned to the window to retrieve a bag from the cashier. "Here, do you want to fix these up while I drive?"

"Where'd the reporters go?"

"Most of them camped out on the common, next to the bandstand."

"Great." She laid a burger in her lap and tried to fold the wrapper back with one hand.

"Hold on a sec." Brian put the directional signal on and pulled into an empty parking lot. "Here, let me do that." He opened two burgers and set an order of fries between them.

Maddie nibbled on a fry. "This whole thing is such a mess."

"So, is it his baby?"

*Just tell him.* "Yes."

"Son of a bitch. I'm going to kill that guy when I get my hands on him."

"No, you're not. It's not his fault."

"You're going to tell me you came on to him?" Brian snorted. "Nice try."

Maddie's face reddened. "Nobody came on to anyone. Dr. Carson used Ring's—uhh, well, you know, to fertilize my—oh, jeez, you know what I'm talking about, artificial insemination and neither of us knew about the other."

"Huh? How could Stanford not know?"

"He didn't. I'm carrying Ring Stanford's child because of Dr. Carson. End of discussion." Her raised voice reverberated off the ceiling of the truck cab.

"Okay. I'm sorry. I get it, even though I don't want to." Brian took a bite of his hamburger and chewed in silence.

Maddie let him. It was a lot to take in. She slid a hand under her burger to lift it, only to have most of its condiments slide out and land on the wrapper in her lap. She set the burger down again.

"I'll help you."

A tear slipped from the corner of Maddie's eye to run down her cheek, followed by another. "No, I can do it." She tossed the bun top into the now empty bag and set it aside, breaking off a piece of the ground beef.

"I'm not talking about the burger." He paused. "I'll do whatever you need me to."

She finished chewing and swiped at her eyes with a paper napkin. "Thanks." She sniffed. "I can't go home right now, I just can't."

"Do you want to stay with us?"

Madison shook her head. "Thanks, but that won't work either. Let me think a moment." It took another bite of burger and three fries before she spoke again. "I have an idea, but I'll need your help."

"I told you I'd help."

She gave him a weak smile and popped two more French fries into her mouth. "You may change your mind before we're done."

"Not a chance."

"Okay, I need clothes."

"No problem, we'll go to University Mall."

"The thing is, I don't want to be spotted in the stores. You'll have to go in and buy some things for me."

"What? Maddie, what do I know about buying women's clothes? Especially a pregnant woman. No one's going to spot you. I think you're being paranoid."

"Oh really? Well, in both Cancun and Boston the story was all over the televisions in the airports. That pretty much makes anyone with a cell phone potential paparazzi. I had to hide in the ladies' room until just before they called the flight." She picked up another fry. "Why do you think I'm starving?"

"Maddie, I think you're tired and stressed. How about you go in and pick out a few things, and I promise I won't let anyone take your picture. I promise."

She exhaled a shaky breath. "All right."

Two hours later, Madison stood outside the Greyhound bus station as Brian tucked a new suitcase under the bus.

"Are you sure you want to do this? With that arm? I'll drive you wherever you want to go."

"I'll be fine. I can change the dressing and most of the stitches will dissolve." She headed to the steps.

"Wait." He put a hand on her arm. "You said you're tired. Why don't you stay over one night and get some rest?"

Madison shook her head. "No, I'll be fine. I bought a prepaid cell phone like you asked; I promise I'll call you as soon as I get there."

"Get where? Why won't you tell me which stop you're getting off at?"

His sigh of exasperation tugged at her heart strings. "Brian, I'll be fine."

"What am I supposed to tell Sherri?"

"Just tell her I had to get away for a while."

"I don't like any of this. Maddie, please come home with me. I won't let anyone near you. I swear. Not even Stanford."

Madison shook her head and reached up to hug him with her uninjured arm. "I've got to go." She climbed the first step. "I'll call you later."

"Maddie, please, I don't want—"

"I'll be fine. Don't worry," she cut him off.

He shook his head and stood outside by the bus as the driver shut the luggage compartment doors and climbed aboard. The door slammed shut.

She blew Brian a kiss and gave a small wave. He raised a hand. *I'm going to miss you and Sherri so much. I just want to go home and rest.* She pushed the thought away as the bus rumbled east.

# Chapter 17

"Who's that?"

"Try to get a picture!"

Ring Stanford rolled over and looked at the alarm clock. 6 AM. *Why can't these guys give it a rest?* It was bad enough Maddie wouldn't talk to him, but the press wasn't helping the situation. They were still outside the compound. Doors slammed and more shouts. *What the hell is going on?*

He pulled on a pair of gym shorts and a polo shirt. "Dave?" No answer. He walked into the kitchen. His manager was nowhere to be seen. *Maybe he's out on the porch.* Ring opened the glass door and stepped onto the large porch only to find it empty. *Maybe he's next door with Sherri and Maddie. Madison's got to talk to me. We can work this out. The sooner, the better.*

Ring headed that way. Almost to the porch, he noticed the slight indent of footprints in the receding surf. *Did one of those bastards get inside the compound? We're going to have to get some security here.* He stopped to listen. The noise out in the street had died down. *I hope Maddie didn't go out there again.* He hurried up the porch steps and pushed aside the bamboo curtain. Two coffee

---

cups sat on the table. He stepped through the door and headed toward the living room when he found the kitchen empty. "Is she—" The question died on his lips.

"Hello, darling." Anne Reese Miller greeted him, her perfectly painted lips curved in a smile as she lounged in an overstuffed club chair. "Surprised to see me?"

"Surprised is not the word I'd use." Ring's tone was cold. He looked from Madison's closed bedroom door to Dave and Sherri, who sat perched on the edge of the sofa opposite Anne. Sherri shook her head.

"I know you're on vacation, but surely you can do better than the beach bum look, especially with the press waiting to get a picture." Anne studied her long red nails a moment. "Remember? First rule—always look the part." And she did. Despite the early morning hour, she wore a sleek black suit with red accents and black heels. "You could at least shave."

"What do you want, Anne?"

"Why to help you, of course, darling."

"To help me? That's a first, and why would I need your help?"

"Well, it would seem you slept with Suzy Homemaker." Her words matched Ring's sarcastic tone. "Though for the life of me, I can't see why—but for argument's sake, we'll say you did, and now she's claiming to have your child."

Sherri jumped up. "Now, just a minute here. You have no right to talk about Maddie that way."

Anne turned a narrowed gaze on the other woman.

Dave grabbed Sherri's hand. "Ahh, I could use another cup of coffee."

"What? Coffee? Now? Who does she think she is? Did you hear what she said?"

"Yeah, I did. Ring will handle it." Dave pulled Sherri in the direction of the kitchen.

Anne watched them walk away and shook her head. "Where'd Dave get her? I hope he's not serious."

Ring remained silent.

"Really, Ring, how could you fall for that kind of thing in this day and age, when you can buy birth control in the dollar store?"

"This is none of your business."

"Of course it is. Someone else is claiming to be Mrs. Ring Stanford. That's my title."

"Not for much longer. I hope you brought signed divorce papers with you."

"Why no, Ring, I'm sorry, I didn't." She went back to studying her nails for a moment. "I completely forgot about them."

"Sure you did. Just sign the damn papers, Anne." Ring laid a hand along the back of his neck and twisted his head to flex muscles. "What are you doing here? Really?" He didn't bother to hide the exasperation in his voice.

"Relax, darling." Anne rose and came to stand close to Ring. "I have good news. Our time apart has given me time to think. I realize now, I was wrong to leave you." She paused. "But I was young and scared. I've grown up a lot since then."

"You didn't look too scared when I found you in bed with Von Timber."

"What can I say? I was confused." She laid a hand on his arm. "But I know what I want now."

"So, now we get to it." Ring shook her hand off and moved to the cold fireplace. "What else do you want, Anne? I already said you can have the Malibu house."

"The beach house is nice." She followed. "But what I want is to be with you. To have a family."

*What?* Anne's expensive perfume enveloped him as she ran a nail down his chest. "You want children?" His gaze landed on the bits of sea glass spread out on the mantle he and Madison had collected.

Anne smiled up at him. "Well, maybe someday—but for now, since you already have a baby on the way, wouldn't it make more sense to get custody of that one when it's born."

"What?" Ring took a step back.

"Well, we could sue for custody. I'm sure it wouldn't take much to get her declared unfit."

"What?" *Is Maddie awake? Can she hear this?* He expected the bedroom door to fly open at any moment.

"Think about it, we'll be a real family." Anne stepped closer still and slipped her arms around him.

For the first time, Ring noticed her dilated pupils and the dark circles under her eyes, cleverly disguised with makeup. "You're using."

She shrugged. "Just a little. Not nearly as much as before. A few pick-me-ups during the day. You know how it is."

"No, I don't." The familiar scent of her perfume now cloyed in his nostrils. He pulled away. "I'm not suing Madison for custody of the baby. She'll be a good mother."

"And I wouldn't?"

"You're a drug addict."

"Name somebody we know who isn't using a little something these days? It comes with the business." She opened her purse, pulled out a cigarette and put it to her lips.

"Don't light that in here."

"What? Light it? It's an e-cig."

"I don't care what it is. Put it away. It's not good for—" He stopped.

"Not good for who?"

"Never mind. Just don't."

"Fine." She dropped it back in her bag and tapped a finger on her cheek. "Something's not right here. You have a fling with little Miss Nobody and now she's mother of the year? Where'd you meet her anyway?"

Ring said nothing, just glanced at the bedroom door.

Anne's eyes narrowed to slits. "Is she here? She's here, isn't she?" She headed toward the bedroom. "Well, I need to meet this paragon of motherhood."

"Leave her out of this." *Relax. The door's locked.* But to Ring's chagrin, the knob turned under Anne's hand, and she swung the door wide.

"Hello?" Anne called and stepped into the room. "Hello? Are you hiding?"

Ring followed. The room was empty. He checked the bathroom. Empty. Two envelopes sat on the nightstand.

"Well, it seems your little birdie has flown the coop. No matter. I'll find her. You can thank me later." With that, Anne Reese Miller walked out of the room.

Ring paid no attention as he ripped open the envelope and studied the folded piece of paper inside for a moment before dropping down to the edge of the bed. *She's gone.*

# Chapter 18

"Ring, it's been two weeks, she's not coming back to Northam. Let's go home. You can get some work done while we wait. I can't keep trying to reschedule everything." Dave waited for Ring to respond. He didn't.

"Fine. Whatever. You're the boss." Dave stared at the neon sign over the bar as he took a sip of his drink. "I wonder what L& L stands for?"

Ring shrugged as the burly bartender set their drinks on the table with more force than necessary, sending a few drops of alcohol over the rim of the glasses to splatter on the table. "Anything else?"

Ring met the man's hostile stare head on. "Just keep our tab open, please."

The man grunted and turned away, only to turn back a moment later. "You know, Madison O'Neill is a real good lady." He unbuttoned the sleeve of his flannel shirt and took his time rolling it up to his elbow. The motion exposed a hairy, muscular forearm. "When my Georgie started school, he had a real hard time, and everybody said I should ship him off to a special school. Everybody but Miss O'Neill. She worked extra with him until she figured it out. Now, with his hearing aids, he keeps right up with the rest of the kids." The man took his time rolling up the other sleeve and stood with fists resting at his thick waist line. "I'd hate to see anyone hurt her."

"You tell 'em, Sandy. That goes double for me," a grizzled man piped up from the next table. "Then I'd have to hurt 'em, 'cause Maddie's a good 'un, just like her daddy and momma before her—always willing to help out if someone was down on their luck." The little man drained the last bit of foam in his glass and scratched at his overgrown beard. "It ain't right. No party this year, no Christmas dinner with all that good food. I walked by her house on the way over here. It's all dark—not even one light. I tell ya, Sandy, it just ain't right." The man's words ended in a grumble as his rheumy gaze landed on Ring. "And I'm pretty sure I know why."

Ring returned his stare. "I have Madison's best interests at heart."

"Bull." The old man turned in his chair to face Ring. "If you did, you'd take that pack of jackal reporters with you and clear out of town, so Maddie can come home."

"Now, Albert, it's not really Mr. Stanford's fault the reporters are here." Matthew Whitman materialized by the table with another man in tow. "I'm not only chairman of the bank, but the mayor of Northam as well; and I can tell you, the influx of people has been good for local business."

*What does he want?*

"You're just as full of bull as he is, Junior Whitman—you always have been."

"Albert, how many times have I asked you to call me Matthew?"

"Obviously, not enough, Junior." The old man's words were dry.

Matthew Whitman shook his head and turned to Ring. "As soon as I got your call today, I contacted Ted. I'm not sure if you remember, but this is Theodore Stoneman, you met him at the Harvest Ball. He owns Stoneman Realty."

With a grunt, the realtor extended a hand. "Nice to see you again, Mr. Stanford. Matthew told me you're ready to look at some real estate."

The pudgy man's announcement caused a low murmur of whispers as several sets of eyes turned their way. *What the hell? This is no one's business but mine.* "I said I was thinking about it and wanted the name of an agent."

Despite Ring's glare, the realtor continued on. "Well, I went one better and came to you. That's the kind of personalized service I provide for elite clientele." The chunky man fumbled around the inside of his sweater vest and tugged out a handkerchief to mop his brow. "Whew, you've got it hot enough in here, Sandy." With each word he spoke, the man's chin folded over his polka dot bow tie. "We have several well appointed properties, any one of which I'm sure you'd find suitable."

"What? You're moving here?" Albie jumped up, his old overcoat bagging open to expose the three sweaters he wore underneath.

"Albert, stay out of this. It's really not your concern."

"Like hell it's not, Junior." The man waved a bony finger at the two businessmen. "I paddled both your backsides more than once when you were kids, and don't think I'm so old I can't knock you on 'em now."

Matthew Whitman's face colored as he cleared his throat. "I'm sorry, Mr. Stanford. Obviously, Albert has had too much to drink."

"I ain't drunk!"

"He's had one beer."

Sandy, the bartender and Albie spoke at the same time.

"We were here when he came in. He's had one beer." Ring spoke up. "But I was just going to invite him to have another with us."

"You were?"

Ring gave Dave a warning glance.

"Right, you were." Dave pulled out a chair. "Have a seat, old timer."

"You were?" The old man scratched his beard again. "Well, that's mighty nice of you."

"Albie, tomorrow's another day." The bartender patted the stooped man's bony shoulder. "Why don't you take Brutus and go on home before it gets dark?"

"But they're goin' to buy me a beer."

"I'll put it on their tab, and you can have it tomorrow. How's that sound?"

Albie made to sit in the empty chair until Sandy caught him under the elbow. "Remember what the doc at the free clinic said? One beer a day?"

"Damn doctors, what do they know? My ticker's fine," Albie muttered. "Okay, okay." He pulled a black and red checkered wool hat, complete with flaps, down over his ears. "Come on, Bru. Let's go home." The hunched man bent a bit lower. A small, but well groomed Pomeranian darted out from under his table and leapt into his arms to lick his face. "This here is Brutus Norstock. The best friend you could ever have." Albie wrapped the lapels of his coat, one over the other, around the dog and held them in place with a warped hand. "I thank you for the beer, but you still can't move here. If you do, Maddie won't ever come back." He turned away and headed toward the door. "See you tomorrow, Sandy. I'll be looking for my beer."

The realtor watched the old man leave, distaste clear on his well-fed features. "I'm sure that's a health code violation—having a dog in here."

"Nope. It's not." Sandy scooped up Albie's empty mug. "He's a service dog. Did you two want something to drink?"

Matthew Whitman cleared his throat. "I think we're all set for now, Sandy."

"Didn't think so." The bartender shook his head and left without another word.

"Now, Mr. Stanford, Theodore brought the details with him on several select properties."

The realtor stepped to the vacant chair next to Ring. "Yes, I think you'll find—"

Ring laid his arm across the back of the empty chair and kept his voice low. "Gentlemen, this is neither the time nor the place. Despite the publicity I've garnered lately, I value my privacy above all else. Anyone who works with me understands that and operates with the utmost discretion." He crooked a finger at the realtor. "Do you understand?"

As the man leaned over the table, his bow tie disappeared all together. "Of course. I understand completely," he whispered. "I'll keep it down. First, I have a property located—"

"Mr.—Stoneman, was it?"

The realtor nodded.

"If I decide to go with your agency, I think this is a conversation better suited to the privacy of your office. Don't you agree?"

"Oh...ahh, of course. Shall I make an appointment for you?" He reached in his pocket to pull out a small notebook. "I have several openings tomorrow and the day after—"

"I'll call you."

"If you'd like. But we could make it right now. I have my appointment book out."

Ring clenched his teeth. "Look, I'll—"

"Gentleman, I'm David Martinez, Mr. Stanford's manager. It's part of my job to keep his schedule. We'll call you soon. Now, if you'll excuse us, we're actually prepping for tomorrow's schedule. Being successful businessmen, I'm sure you understand." Dave gave them an ingratiating smile as he rose and extended a hand. "It was good to meet both of you."

The men had no choice but to shake his hand in farewell. "You'll put me in his appointments, right?" Theodore Stoneman hazarded as he backed away from the table. "Do you need my card?"

Dave tapped his temple with an index finger. "Nope. Got it all right here."

The men left the bar.

"What was that about?"

"I'm going to buy a place here."

"You're kidding—why?"

Ring smoothed a hand over his hair. "'Cause I like it here. I want to be here."

"Even if Maddie isn't here? That old man might be right. She might not come back as long as you're here. It's been two weeks and no one's seen her."

Ring glanced around at the after-work crowd in the bar. "Somebody has to know something. Northam's a small town."

Dave snorted. "Well, if they do, they sure as hell ain't telling you. C'mon, give it up. You look like shit. When was the last time you slept?"

"I don't know."

"Or shaved? Or ate something? Let's go home. You're not doing anyone any good here."

"No. I have to find her. What if something happened?"

"Then you'd know. You've got five guys looking for her."

"Have they checked in today?"

Dave nodded.

"Anything new?"

"No. Just what we already know. She flew into Burlington, Vermont, bought some clothes, took $500.00 out of an ATM and disappeared." Dave smoothed down his mustache. "She's going to have to surface soon. She hasn't used a credit card and $500.00 only goes so far."

"Has Sherri said anything?"

Dave shook his head. "Nope. Though I haven't talked to her that much. That brother of hers is always around nowadays."

The door of the L & L opened to let in a gust of wind and snow, along with Brian Holt.

"Speak of the devil." Dave raised his glass in salute.

Brian glared in their direction before heading to the bar. He slid onto a stool, his back to them.

*He knows something.* Ring studied the man from across the room. "Unless someone's been sending her money." He set his drink down and pushed back his chair.

Dave laid a hand on his arm. "Forget it, man. Sherri says he doesn't know where Maddie is. Even if he did, I'm pretty sure you'd be the last person he'd tell."

Ring's phone buzzed. Several people, including Brian Holt, looked his way as he glanced at the display and then put the phone to his ear. "Look, Anne, I've told you—" He paused to listen. "What? What plan to flush her out? Press conference? What are you talking about? Hello?" He glanced at the phone. "She hung up."

"What's she talking about?"

"She said she was going to help me find the baby."

"I told you she was *loco.*"

"I think you're right. She's got it in her head we should raise the baby."

"We, as in you and her? You're kidding, right? Anne raise a kid? Besides, I can't see Madison going for that." Dave took another sip of his drink. "What was that about a press conference?"

"I have no clue." Ring stood, picked up his drink and tossed it back in one swallow. "Look, go on back if you want, but I can't leave. I got Madison into this mess, and I have to fix it." He inclined his head toward the bar. "Regardless of what Sherri says, I think Holt knows where she is, and I'm going to find out."

"Hey, there's a special report," someone called from down at the end of the bar. "Sandy, turn the T.V. up."

Ring glanced at the television bolted to the wall and his empty glass hit the table. "What the hell?"

On the screen, Anne Reese Miller stepped up to a podium fronted with a multitude of different size microphones. "Good afternoon, ladies and gentlemen. Thank you for coming. This will be brief. The press has always been kind to my husband and myself." A close up on her face focused on a single tear as it slid down her cheek, even as she manifested a tremulous smile.

Dave snorted as Ring dropped back into his chair. "And you said she can't act."

"That is, until a couple of weeks ago, when photos were published showing my husband kissing a pregnant woman. Yes, he did kiss her, and yes, she was pregnant, but there's more to the story. I'm here to clear up any misunderstandings and ask for help." Several reporters jumped up. Anne dabbed at her eyes with a tissue amid a flurry of questions. "The kiss was one of gratitude." She raised a hand for silence. "Please, no questions, this is hard enough."

"What's she up to?" Dave hissed near his ear.

"No good." A knot twisted in the pit of Ring's stomach.

"Yes, gratitude." Anne sniffed. "Sorry, this is so difficult. We've kept our reconciliation quiet until now, but Ring was grateful to her because, unfortunately, I haven't been able to carry a child, and this woman is—was our surrogate." She paused to dab at her eyes again. "And she's disappeared with our baby."

A man stepped forward and placed a large easel next to Anne. A picture of Madison rested on it. "This is the woman who took our baby." Tears now streamed down Anne's cheeks. "Her name is Madison O'Neill. Though she's from New England; she could be anywhere. We're not sure of her mental state, so if you see her, please don't make direct contact. We've set up a tip line." The man to Anne's side set a plaque with a toll free number in block letters on the easel under Madison's picture. "My husband is so distraught he's offered a $50,000 reward to anyone with information that brings our baby back." Anne dabbed at her eyes again. "That's all for now. Thank you." She left the podium amid shouts from the press.

Both men sat stunned.

"I can't believe she just did that." Dave shook his head.

Ring grabbed up his phone. Someone tapped him on the shoulder. He turned.

"You bastard," was all Ring heard before Brian Holt drove a fist into his eye.

# Chapter 19

Maddie pulled the cabin door closed and shivered in her light coat. It had snowed several inches this afternoon. *I've been here two weeks; it was bound to snow sooner or later.* She'd spent most of that time trying to figure out her next move, now that the world knew she was carrying Ring Stanford's child. *I should've never gone with him.* She shook her head. *It's done. Figure out what you're going to do about it.* The only solution she'd come up with was to go home and face everyone. But so far, Maddie hadn't been able to bring herself to call anyone to come and get her.

She paused a moment to check traffic before hurrying across the 4-way intersection to the small convenience store at the other end of the parking lot on the corner.

"Good evening." Madison headed to the cooler at the back of the store. *A dozen eggs. A half gallon of milk.* She waited in line behind an old man chatting with the heavyset woman at the counter.

"Hey, Herb. How are you?"

"Pretty good, Mildred. Finally gettin' some snow, huh?"

"Yup, we're supposed to get some more later on tonight. It's to be expected. It's almost Christmas." She handed the man change. "You got your shoppin' all done?"

*Christmas shopping? I didn't even do any this year.* An unexpected sense of sadness caused tears to well at the thought. *Enough.* Madison swiped at her eyes and glanced at the magazine rack. *Maybe something to read.* Her eyes dropped to several small piles of papers laid out in a row along the bottom shelf. *A newspaper?*

"Yup. All wrapped and under the tree. Better be done, seein' how it's only a few days 'til Christmas. How about you?"

Madison blinked and stepped closer to the magazine rack. REWARD. Her own image stared back at her from the front of one of the newspapers. *Last year's school picture?*

"Yup. All ready. See ya tomorrow."

"See ya, Herb." The woman turned in Madison's direction. "Can I help you find something?"

Maddie snatched up the small pile of papers, folded them in half and tucked them under her arm before straightening to return the woman's curious smile. "I'm all set. Thanks." She stepped to the counter.

"Not a problem." The woman hesitated a moment. "How are you doing this evening?"

Madison kept her smile in place. "I'm fine, thank you."

"Good. Are you due soon?"

Maddie nodded.

"Well, you be careful out there—that snow is slippery. Okay, the milk and eggs?"

"Yes."

"And the paper? It looks like you got several copies there. Did you want them all?"

Maddie blushed, but left the papers where they were. "Ah, yes. Sorry. I have four newspapers."

The cashier rang them up. "Must be something special in them."

"No. No," Madison stammered. "I, ahh, need more paper to start the stove."

"Oh, well, in that case, I've got some old ones back here you can use. No sense wasting your money."

"No. No. That's fine." Maddie paid and left the store to hurry back to her cabin. She'd come to northern Vermont because it was remote and quiet in the Kingdom at this time of year. Summer people were gone from their camps and the snowmobilers wouldn't be here in force for another few weeks.

She closed the door, turned on a lamp and scanned the front page of the newspaper. *Surrogate? This is my baby! Why would Ring offer $50,000? He's back with his wife? Is he going to try and take the baby?*

An hour of pacing brought no answers. To take her mind off it, Maddie put together the quiche she'd planned for dinner and slipped it in the oven only to find when it was done she had no appetite.

She glanced at the clock on the wall. "I'm going to bed. I'll be able to think better after a good night's sleep." She slipped into her nightgown and crawled under several quilts. After much tossing and turning, Madison finally drifted off.

*"You can't have my baby. I won't let you."*

*"Don't be silly. Of course I can."* Anne Reese Miller laughed. *"I want Ring. He wants this baby, so I want this baby. And trust me, I always get what I want. Bye now."*

*"No, you can't. You can't..."*

"You can't take my baby!" Maddie sat upright in bed. It was dark in the room. She sighed and rested a hand on her abdomen. "A dream. Just a dream. Thank goodness." She took a couple of more deep breaths before pushing back the blankets. "I have to find out what's going on. Who can I call?" *Brian? Sherri?* "No, they won't know about this. Face it, you have to call him." She glanced at the clock. Almost 10 PM. *He should be awake and if not, too bad. It won't hurt him to lose a little sleep.* Maddie dug in her purse for the dog-eared business card and picked up the telephone before she changed her mind.

He answered on the first ring. "Hello?"

"Hi, it's Madison."

"Madison? Where are you? Are you all right?"

"I'm fine, no thanks to you."

"Thank goodness you called. I've been going crazy. Look, I need to talk to you; some things have happened."

"Things? Like I'm your surrogate?"

"Madison, I didn't have anything to do with that."

"Really? What about the money? Did you put a bounty on me?"

"What? No."

"Are you so desperate for this baby, you'd put your wife up to lying? Boy, was I a fool."

"This was all Anne."

"Just tell me—are you back with her?"

"No." He hesitated. "But she's got it in her head we should get back together."

Maddie thought of her nightmare and swallowed back the lump in her throat at his words. "Well, good. I hope it works out for you."

"Madison, it's not like that. I haven't been with her in a long time." He paused. "I don't want to be with her."

"She's beautiful. How can you say that?"

"Because," he exhaled. "Because I want to be with you."

*What? He's choosing me over Anne Reese Miller?* Butterflies churned in the pit of Maddie's stomach. Her gaze landed on the newspaper she'd tossed on the coffee table earlier. *Wake up, it's a trick.* "Sorry, but I find that hard to believe." She swallowed again. "And you might as well know, I'm not giving up my baby."

"Madison, please, give me a chance."

"We already tried that once. Mexico, remember? That didn't work out so well."

"I swear, I won't let anyone take our baby from you."

"You said you didn't put up the money."

"I didn't, but nobody knows that. Please tell me where you are."

"I don't know what to do." She sank to the couch. "What if this is a trick?"

"It's no trick, I swear." He let out a gust of breath. "Okay, look, if you don't want me in the baby's life when this is over, I promise—I'll bow out."

"You'd do that? Just walk away? Really?"

"I don't want to, but yes, I would."

Maddie sighed and glanced out the window. Snowflakes drifted in the glow of the parking lot lights. *What should I do?*

"Please tell me where you are. I need to get you some place safe."

"Safe? What are you talking about? I'm safe."

"Madison, I don't want to scare you, but I'm sure there are people looking for you—people willing to do anything for a lot less than $50,000. I don't want you hurt. Please think about the baby." There was silence for a few moments. "Madison?"

"Okay."

"Okay? Great." His words oozed relief. "Where are you?"

"The Northeast Kingdom."

"A kingdom? How'd you get out of the country on five hundred dollars?"

"What are you talking about? I'm in northern Vermont."

"Oh, good. Give me directions. I'll be there shortly."

"I don't know where you are, but it's the middle of the night. I'll call Brian in the morning. He can be here in a couple of hours, depending on the weather."

"So can I."

"What? Where are you?"

"In Northam."

"What are you doing there?"

"Looking for you."

"Fine." She gave him directions. "But wait until morning, please. It's snowing. The roads are going to get bad."

"Don't worry about it, it'll be fine."

"No, it won't be fine. That limo is no match for the roads here. Promise me."

"Madison, it'll be—"

"Promise me." She waited.

"Fine. I promise not to bring the limo out."

"Good." A yawn escaped her lips followed by a shiver. "I'm going back to bed. I'll talk to you tomorrow." She hung up and yawned again. *Did I do the right thing?* She glanced at the front door. *Is someone really looking for me?* She padded over to the portal and flipped the dead bolt before crawling back in bed.

A howling wind pulled Madison from slumber. *The storm must be bad.* The windows began to rattle as a deep vibration shook the small building. *What's going on?* Maddie hurried through the house and pulled open the front door as a loud whirring sound filled the air. She tried to ignore the bite of cold as she waded through snow drifts on the porch to get to the railing, craning her neck skyward. An onslaught of turbulence swirled the falling snow, covering her in a fine layer. *What is that?*

Madison had her answer a moment later as a shiny black helicopter set down under the lights in the parking lot across the street. She shivered in her thin nightgown but didn't move. After several minutes, a man in a khaki jump suit came around and slid open a door on the side. Ring Stanford jumped out and hurried across the street, bag in hand. Maddie stared in disbelief.

Ring hustled up the steps. "Are you all right?"

Madison looked from him to the helicopter and back to him again. Twice. And still couldn't find her voice.

"Are you hurt?" He stepped close.

She took a step back.

"Madison. What's wrong? Has something happened? Do you need—"

"Really?" She sputtered and pointed across the street. Several people had climbed out of a newly arrived car and circled the aircraft in curiosity. Someone exclaimed, "Cool!"

"A helicopter? Really?"

"What?" Ring shrugged with a look of innocence on his face.

"Mr. Stanford?" The man in the jumpsuit stood at the bottom of the steps. "There's already more snow than predicted, and it's not letting up. It looks like we're grounded 'til morning." He hesitated. "The price is still fifteen, right?"

Maddie stepped back to the rail. "You flew in this weather for fifteen hundred dollars?"

"No, ma'am. Fifteen thousand," the man said with a soft southern drawl. "But I admit I wouldn't want to try it again right away." The pilot headed down the walkway. "If you're looking for me, I rented the cabin next door for the night. I'll see you in the morning."

Maddie waited for the man to enter the building and close the door. "Did he really just say fifteen thousand, Ring?" Maddie shook her head in disbelief. "You couldn't bring the limo tomorrow?"

"I told you I wouldn't bring the limo tonight. I kept my word." His smile was sheepish. "Anyway, it seems both of the limos were previously booked. And though I tried, no amount of money could dissuade the bride to give one up. The chopper ended up being faster." Ring shivered. "Don't you think we've stood out here long enough? You don't even have a coat on. Are you wearing slippers?"

She nodded, still unable to comprehend he was here.

"You're all wet. You're going to get a chill."

Another car had arrived in the parking lot, and now the whole group stared their way with interest.

*What are people doing out at this time of night in a snow storm?* "Let's get inside before someone figures out who you are." Still shaking her head, Maddie reentered the cabin followed by Ring and kicked off her soggy slippers by the door. "Honestly, what were you thinking?"

Ring ignored Madison's glare as she stood with hands on hips. "You're all wet. You need to get out of that nightgown before you get sick. Do you have a robe?"

"I have another nightgown in the top drawer of the bureau."

Ring was back in a moment to find she hadn't moved. "Madison, your nightgown is wet; you need to change."

"I know." She worked at the buttons at the collar of the gown with shaking fingers. "Turn around, please."

"What? Madison, at a time like this—"

"Turn around."

Ring shook his head but presented his back, and Maddie shed the sodden material, using his shoulder to steady herself. A moment later, she muttered, "Darn it."

"What?"

"Youch. My arm. Can you help me, please?"

Ring spun around. Madison had the nightgown on, the hem to her knees, but one sleeve caught the bandage on her arm, lifting the edge.

"Hold still." He worked the sleeve down, allowing the nightgown to drop around her ankles.

"Thank you." She smoothed down the material, unaware the motion accentuated her pregnancy.

Ring noticed. His throat tightened at the sight and he had to clear it before speaking. "Hold on." He grabbed a small fleece blanket and stepped closer, covering her shoulders. He held the ends of the blanket together between them. "Thank you for calling me," he whispered.

She met his gaze. "Thank you for coming."

Ring lowered his head until his lips touched hers in a soft kiss as his arms slid around her. "I've missed you so much." His arms tightened. "We can make this work."

"Ring, I don't know—"

He silenced her with another kiss. "We can."

A shiver shook her from head to toe. "Sorry. I seem to have caught a chill."

"We need to get you warmed up. I think you should get back in bed."

She acquiesced. "That's probably a good idea. It's been a long day."

Ring nodded and tucked her in. "Good night, Madison." He gave her a lingering kiss before backing away from the bed.

"What about you?"

"I'm going to stay up a while longer."

"I'll come back out and sit with you." She made to flip the covers back.

"No, stay in bed. I'll see you in the morning." He closed the door.

Two hours later, Ring shifted again, trying to stay awake and find a comfortable position on the hard couch at the same time. The lights were out and the only sounds in the cabin were the ping of sleet against the windows and the crackle of wood in the stove. The small black bag he'd brought in sat near his feet, Dave's gun inside. *Just in case.*

"Ring?"

He jumped. "Madison, why are you out of bed? Is something wrong?"

"No." She came to stand in front of the wood stove to warm her hands. The light from the glass front of the stove outlined her body through her nightgown.

Ring swallowed.

She eased onto the sofa next to him. "I can't sleep." She shivered.

He pulled an afghan from the back of the sofa and tucked it around her.

"What am I going to do about this, Ring?"

"About what?"

"Denseness doesn't suit you," Madison sighed. "About this—this whole thing. The reporter taking pictures was bad enough, but then your wife saying I'm a surrogate. Why would she do that?"

Ring shook his head. "She's got some problems."

"Yes, but now they're my problems," Maddie's voice was quiet as she studied her hands. "So, what am I supposed to do?"

"Right now, nothing but rest. Dave's working with my publicists to come up with a statement."

"That says what? Your wife is telling a lie? Or that the baby is yours and mine? Anything you say will just make it worse."

"I'm sorry this all happened, Madison." He yawned. "Sorry. I haven't had much sleep." He reached over and clasped her hand. "We'll figure this out. I promise. In Mexico, we were—"

"Ring, our time in Mexico was like a dream, but this is real life. And my life's never going to be the same."

"It'll be different, but it doesn't mean it's going to be bad. Life is change." A few moments passed as he studied her in the firelight. "What do you want to do?"

"I don't know." Her wistful smile held sadness. "No, that's not true. I know I have to go back home. I just hate facing everyone, so I've been putting it off. But I miss home and everyone in Northam. It's only a few days until Christmas. Do you know, I've never missed a Christmas at home?" She sniffed. "My family has always done the Christmas party—most everyone in town comes."

"Is that what you want?"

"I want to be home."

"Then we'll go back to Northam tomorrow morning."

"Just like that?"

He caught the glisten of tears on her cheeks, and put an arm around her shoulders to give a gentle squeeze. "Just like that."

She gave him a look of doubt.

"I'm sorry about what happened in Mexico and about what Anne did." He paused. "And I'm sorry for all the crazy things that have happened since I came into your life. But regardless of what the world thinks, neither of us have done anything wrong. Let me take you home, please."

"How am I supposed to face everyone?"

"What are you talking about? If there's anything I've learned from my short time in Northam—regardless of who the baby's father is, the people there love you."

She shook her head and swiped at her eyes.

"It's true. Albert Norstock was ready to take me on in the L & L."

"You met Albie? And Brutus?" Despite her tears, a slight smile touched Madison's lips at his nod. "Is that where your black eye came from?"

Several moments passed. "No, this was courtesy of your friend—Brian Holt."

"What? What happened?"

"It doesn't matter now." He raised her hand and brought it to his lips, holding her gaze with his dark eyes. "Madison, do you want to go home?"

The tears continued. "Yes," she whispered. "But I don't know how it's going to—"

Ring put a finger to her lips. "Shh. It'll work. Now, why don't you get some rest? Come on, back to bed with you." He yawned and rose to stretch before leading her back to the bedroom.

"Where are you going?"

"Back to the sofa."

"You should lay down too. You look exhausted."

"I will."

"You might as well stretch out here. There are extra blankets and it's more comfortable than the couch."

"You don't mind?"

Maddie shook her head.

He left the room.

"Ring?"

He was back in a moment, dropping the black bag onto the floor by the bed. He laid down on top of the blankets and pulled a quilt up before wrapping an arm around her, fitting himself to her back and placing a tender kiss on the nape of her neck.

The softness of the bed and the warmth emanating from her closeness lulled Ring. He sighed and drifted, only to start awake and glance at the alarm clock. *2 AM.* He slid off the bed, and went to the living room to lift the telephone receiver and punch in a number. "Hi, it's me. No, I've been here a while, but we can talk about it later. Listen, we're coming back tomorrow. I need you to do some things." Ring hung up the phone half an hour later and eased back onto the bed, pulling Madison close again.

# Chapter 20

The next afternoon, Maddie sat in the back of the limo with Ring next to her as the heavy car wielded its way over slushy, but mostly clear roads.

The pilot had waited until Ring paid him this morning to inform them it might not be the best thing for Madison to fly at this advanced stage of her pregnancy. It was okay with Madison. She wasn't sure she was ready for her first helicopter ride yet.

After a while the scenery on the highway became familiar as the partition between front and back slid down to reveal the driver and another man in the front seat. The passenger glanced over his shoulder at them. "We should arrive in approximately ten minutes, sir." The hooded sweatshirt he wore seemed in sharp contrast with his close cropped hair and sunglasses.

Ring nodded.

The dark glass barrier slid closed without a sound.

Madison turned to Ring. "Who's that guy in front with the driver?"

"Just a friend." Ring looked out the window.

"A friend that calls you sir? I don't think so."

He turned to meet her gaze. "Fine. He's security—just in case."

"In case of what?"

"Anything." A moment later, the limo glided to a stop at the end of the exit ramp. Ring clasped her hand. "It'll be fine. It's just a precaution."

*Northam. I'm back home.* Maddie scooted forward a little on the seat, her relief mixed with apprehension as they neared the center of town. She scanned the area through tinted windows. "You know, we could've probably gone unnoticed if we were in an SUV or anything other than this."

He shrugged. "I'll consider that next time." His dry tone told Maddie he'd do no such thing. "Relax."

"How can I relax? The town is crawling with reporters..." They passed the town common. Though there were numerous tire tracks in the snow and several overflowing garbage cans next to the bandstand, the lot was empty. "Where'd they go? Did you do something to them?"

Ring put up his hands. "I can do a lot, but getting rid of the paparazzi? Unfortunately, even I haven't mastered that trick, or I would've used it a long time ago." He glanced out the back window as they moved on, curiosity clear on his features. "I have no idea where they're hiding."

A moment later, they pulled onto Madison's road. Both sides of the street were lined with cars. She craned her neck to see out the window to no avail. "What's going on?"

The car slowed and pulled into a driveway. *My driveway.* She grabbed the door handle.

"Madison, you should wait for—"

Ring's words were lost as she exited the car only to stop, too stunned to speak. *Someone decorated.* The large spruce tree on the lawn glowed with lights. Green wreaths with large red bows adorned every window as well as the lamp post at the bottom of the steps. But it was the porch itself that drew Madison's attention. The front porch teemed with people.

Albie Norstock rested one hand on the porch rail as he gave a vigorous wave. "Hi, Maddie. Welcome home."

Madison smiled and waved back as she looked from face to face. Winona and Tom Evans. Sandy from the L & L. Willa Mae. Fred Edgars and his mom. Some of her students. Dave Martinez. Sherri and Brian. Maddie's vision blurred as tears welled.

Ring joined her on the path and leaned close to her ear. "Merry Christmas, Madison."

She turned to him as tears openly flowed now. "What's this?"

"I believe it's your annual holiday party."

"What? You're kidding?"

He shook his head. "Shall we?" He guided her up the steps and onto the porch.

"It's so good to see you all." She hugged everyone within arm's length. "It's cold out here. How about we go inside? I can at least make some hot chocolate and popcorn."

Everyone smiled and clapped.

Sherri came to stand by her. "I've missed you."

"I've missed you too." Their hug was brief as the group worked its way through the front door. "We'll talk, okay?"

Sherri nodded. "Sure. Now let's get inside since it's not likely to get any warmer out here. Oh, do I miss Mexico."

Madison laughed, looped a hand around Sherri's arm and walked through the door to her second shock of the day. Someone had decorated the house on the inside as well. Cream and gold decorations and small white lights were everywhere Maddie looked.

Music drifted in from the parlor. Madison stepped over to the doorway, taking Sherri with her. The room was devoid of furniture, but more decorations in the same color scheme graced the room, including a twelve-foot tree in the corner. A small table was set up in the opposite corner, flanked by speakers.

A man with headphones looked up. "How ya doin'?"

"Fine." She turned to Sherri and whispered, "Where's all my furniture?"

Sherri grinned. "Safe. Don't worry."

A huge wreath hung over the living room fireplace. Madison skirted a large group of people to glance into the dining room. A portable bar, complete with bartender occupied one wall. Cream colored linens and gorgeous gold centerpieces covered several tables laden with artistically arranged food. She turned in a circle. The white lights gave the whole house a warm intimate feel. *The old place looks great, like a grand dame bejeweled for an elegant affair.* "I can't believe you did all—"

"I didn't. Well, Dave and I helped, but," Sherri pointed over Madison's shoulder. "It was all him."

Maddie turned to look across the room. Ring stood in front of the fireplace talking to Chief Lawson. He glanced her way and smiled. She returned the smile.

Sherri tugged on her arm. "I'm starved. Let's get something to eat and find a place to sit, then we can talk."

They filled plates and found two chairs near the front windows of the living room. Madison ate little of the food as one person after another stopped to talk to her. Though she knew people were curious about her situation, no one mentioned it as they chatted about family, work, anything but what was happening in Madison's life.

"Hey, Maddie."

"Brian." She rose and wrapped her arms around him. He squeezed her in return. They stayed this way for several moments until she caught a movement out of the corner of her eye. *Who's out on the front porch? A reporter?* She pulled back, but Brian kept an arm around her shoulders.

"How are you?"

She smiled up at him. "I'm good."

"Really?"

She glanced across the room to find Ring Stanford watching them. "Really."

"Are you home to stay?"

She nodded.

"Good. It's about time things started getting back to normal around here."

A shadow passed in front of the window again. "Who's out on the porch? It's freezing out." Madison pulled back the lace curtain with caution. A man with short hair and in a heavy coat with the collar turned up nodded to her before continuing to scan the area in front of the house as he moved. *More security.* She dropped the curtain and sighed. "I guess it depends on your version of normal."

"Do you want me to ask them to leave?"

"No, it's okay. Let's just enjoy this."

"Hi Brian. Welcome back, Madison."

Maddie glanced up to find Mina Miller holding a small bundle in a blue blanket. "Hi, Mina. You had the baby?"

Mina nodded.

Sherri stood. "Take my seat, I'm going to get some more food."

"Thank you." Mina sat on the edge of the chair. "Sam is at the dessert table getting ice cream with the other kids. They should be here shortly." She smiled. "Providing they don't talk him into seconds. They know he's a pushover."

Maddie laughed. "He loves his kids all right."

"Would you like to hold the baby?"

"I'd love to."

Mina set the baby in her arms. Tiny red fists tucked under the sleeping baby's chin. "When did you have him?"

"Three weeks ago."

*When I was in Mexico.* Maddie drank in the baby—downy, dark hair and all. "Oh, he's perfect. What'd you name him?"

"Orrin George. After Sam's brother and my father. Of course, we call him Ori."

Madison smiled. "That's perfect."

"Thank you. This is a lovely party, Maddie. The house looks beautiful."

"Thanks, but I can't take the credit." She lifted her eyes to meet Ring's serious countenance as he studied her from across the room. Dave tapped him on the shoulder, and it was several moments before Ring shifted his attention to his manager.

"Hi, Maddie. What do you think of our son? Handsome fellow, huh?" Sam Miller stood next to Brian.

"He is." Madison laid a light kiss on the baby's forehead.

"Ahh, Sam, where are the rest of our children?"

"I've got it under control, Mrs. Miller." Sam grinned. "They're having a teeny bit more ice cream with Laurie and Hank."

"Sam! More? They're never going to sleep tonight."

"Aww, come on, give 'em a break. It's Christmas." He turned to Brian. "Hey, did you hear someone is looking to buy the old Addison Place?"

Brian shook his head. "That place is a wreck."

"Exactly. Which means it'll be good work for us and lots of it."

"Maybe." Brian rubbed a hand across his chin. "Who bought it?"

The baby started to squirm in Madison's arms.

"I'll take him." Sam lifted the baby and settled him against his shoulder, his large hand gently patting the baby's back. "Nobody seems to know for sure, but I heard it was a woman from New York or New Jersey. It couldn't hurt to bid on it if the work comes out."

"Agreed."

"Well, look at this—the gang's all here."

*Oh no. Willa Mae.* Maddie plastered a smile on her face. "Hi, Willa Mae. How are Marv and the kids?"

"Okay, I guess. They're around here someplace." Willa Mae snorted. "You know Marv likes comin' here every year; he's not one to miss a chance for free food. So, how're you feelin', Maddie?"

"I'm good, Willa Mae."

"Mmm. Good." The woman slapped a hand on Brian's back. "Well, I guess I can't yank your chain about bein' the baby's daddy anymore."

"Willa." Brian's one word carried a warning.

Several people looked their way with curiosity.

Maddie's face flamed. "If you'll excuse me just a minute." She rose and headed for the kitchen.

"What? What's wrong? I didn't say nothin' about the rich Hollywood guy."

Tonight, the French doors between the living room and kitchen were closed. Madison pushed through to find Ring and Dave Martinez sitting at the kitchen table, several pieces of paper between them. "I'm sorry. I didn't mean to interrupt."

Sherri followed right behind her. "She didn't mean anything by it; you know how Willa is."

"What happened? Is everything okay?" Concern etched Ring's features.

"Fine." Madison moved closer to the table. "Hi, Dave. What's going on?"

"We're just going over how to handle Anne's claims." Ring pulled out a chair.

"And?" Madison sat down between the two men as Sherri came to stand by Dave.

Dave glanced at Ring.

"Go ahead."

"Well, I talked to Jerry Rosen, he's Ring's lawyer." Dave explained. "He said we could threaten to hit Anne with a defamation suit unless she retracts her statement. But," Dave held up an index finger and then pointed at Madison. "Be prepared. Her lawyers might turn around and slap a law suit on you."

Maddie laid a hand on her chest. "Me? What'd I do?"

"It's something called an alienation of affection suit. They'll claim you interrupted the marriage."

Maddie groaned.

"Anne and I split up long before I met Madison."

"According to Jerry, it's just a maneuver, but once the tabloids get a hold of it..." Dave shrugged.

"That's crazy." Ring drummed his fingers on the table. "What'd Jerry suggest we do?"

"Well, the fastest way to get rid of the hired guns would be to get Anne to admit publicly she lied about the surrogacy." Dave shook his head. "But knowing Anne, that's a tall order."

"We all know she lied," Maddie sputtered as she pushed back from the table.

"Madison, we'll figure this out." Ring laid a hand on her arm to prevent her from getting up. "I have to figure out how to deal with her without getting you involved—if possible." He tipped his head from side to side a couple of times to flex his neck muscles. "Think, Dave. What's Anne want?"

Dave snorted. "Everything."

"Can you be a bit more specific?" Ring's question oozed sarcasm.

"Okay." David stroked his mustache. "She loves money, that's always a good start."

"We already tried that. What else?"

"I don't know—let me think." A frown marred the swarthy man's brow.

No one said anything for a few moments.

"An Oscar."

All eyes turned toward Sherri.

"Yeah, right, like that's going to happen," Dave scoffed.

"I didn't say it was going to happen. I said it's what she wants."

"What makes you say that?" Ring questioned.

"I didn't say it, she did—in several articles and on a TV interview when she was making that movie Encroachment." Sherri sat down. "She said with Von Timber directing she felt she finally had a chance to win an Oscar—something she'd always wanted."

"Baby, that's a good thought but—"

"No, she's right, Dave. It is what Anne wants. She used to go crazy every time an unfavorable review came out." Ring shook his head. "She said someday she'd show them when the mantle had a whole row of statues."

"Well, boss, unless you've got an extra Oscar laying around, we're screwed."

"We don't have to get her an Oscar, just a chance at one. What's the hottest project going right now?"

Dave leaned back in the chair and crossed his arms. "That's easy. The project you just turned down—Cameron Scott's new film."

Ring grinned and pulled his cell phone from his pocket. "Perfect. I'm giving him a call." He punched a number in on the phone and waited a moment. "Hi, Cam. It's Ring Stanford. What?" He got up and paced to the other side of the room. "No, I didn't change my mind. What? Seventy?" He glanced back at the table a moment before opening the back door. "I really appreciate it, but I can't. Listen, the reason I called. I want to—" He closed the door behind him.

"Seventy million, damn," Dave grumbled as he shook his head.

"Seventy million what? Dollars?"

Dave nodded at Maddie's shocked expression. "Scott really wanted him in this movie, but Ring turned him down."

"Why, if it's such a good opportunity?"

Dave shrugged. "He has his reasons."

*Who turns down seventy million dollars?*

Five minutes later, Ring stepped back into the kitchen with an involuntary shiver. "That's great, Cam. Thanks. What?" He listened for a minute and then smiled. "Definitely. Next time. Bye." He disconnected the phone. "All set."

"What's all set?"

He smiled at Maddie. "He's going to call Anne and offer her a supporting part in the project—with one stipulation. One of the producers wants this surrogacy mess gone pronto, it's not good publicity, or they'll move on to the next name on the list."

Dave frowned. "Which producer? I know everyone on that project, they don't care."

"Me. You're looking at the project's newest backer."

"How much?"

"Just a few million." Ring came to stand at the edge of the table. "Let's see if she takes the bait."

Maddie wrapped an arm around her abdomen. "In the meantime, everyone thinks I'm some kind of crazy surrogate gone awry."

"Not the people who know and love you...and unless I miss my guess, that's everyone in this house right now."

Maddie shook her head. "I can tell by the way everyone is looking at me, they're wondering if the stories are true."

Ring was quiet for a minute as he studied her. "Well, let's tell them."

"About which part? The surrogacy? Or that it's your baby?" Her cheeks flushed hot at the thought.

"For now, the surrogacy. I'd just as soon let everyone know you're having my baby, but I'll leave that part up to you to confirm—if and when you choose to."

"Thank you."

Ring stood and held out a hand. "Are you ready?"

She shook her head. "What? Now?"

"Yes, right now, while everyone is here." His dark eyes held a pleading look. "Madison. Please trust me."

She let out her breath in a gust and placed her hand in his. "Okay."

They returned to the living room. "Everyone," Ring raised his voice to be heard over the murmur of several conversations. "Can we have your attention for a minute?" He turned to Dave. "The music?"

Ring cleared his throat as people quieted down. "Thanks, we'll just take a moment of your time, and then we can get back to the party. First of all, thanks for coming on such short notice."

"Yes, thank you everyone. It's good to be home." Maddie's hesitant smile encompassed the room.

"I'm sure you've all heard bits and pieces of what the world thinks is going on, but we wanted you to know the truth." Ring's expression became serious. "Madison is not a surrogate for my soon-to-be ex-wife, or anyone else for that matter. This is her baby." He paused and looked her way. When she didn't say anything after a moment, he gave a resigned nod. "Okay, thanks, folks. That's it, let's get back to the party."

*I need to tell them. I want to tell them.* "Wait." Madison cleared her throat, straightened her shoulders and leveled her gaze on the crowd. "It's also Ring's baby."

Murmurs sounded throughout the room.

Ring gave Maddie's hand a squeeze. "Now you know. The only other thing I'm going to say about the particulars of this situation is even though neither of us had a hand in this match, after getting to know Madison O'Neill, I couldn't have chosen a better mother for my child." He put an arm around Maddie's shoulders and laid a gentle kiss against her temple as he whispered, "Thank you."

Maddie's cheeks warmed.

He turned to the assembly again. "Madison's been worried that some people might think less of her for what's gone on, though none of it was in her control. But I think," Ring paused. "I've spent enough time here to know that's not true. This town is more than a community—it's a family. And as Maddie's family, I know you'll love and protect her, and keep this quiet. Regardless of what the rest of the world thinks."

Several people spoke up.

"Of course."

"Absolutely."

"Bru and I love ya, Maddie." Albert Norstock worked his way to the front of the crowd, his dog under arm. "We ain't afraid to run them news people off again!"

Ring looked at the little man with skepticism. "You got the reporters to leave?"

"Well, not just me." Albie indicated the people behind him. "We all did."

"How?"

"We had a town meeting and decided it was time to persuade them to move on." This came from Sandy, the burly owner of the L & L.

Dave shook his head and dragged a hand down his mustache. "At least no reporters were killed in the town riot."

"Nope, just a couple of cameras," Chief Lawson spoke up. "But it's amazing how intimidating a whole town armed with everything from bats to mops can be. Those crews were packed up in less than an hour, and I escorted them to the town line." He pushed his cowboy hat to the back of his head. "I can't vouch that more won't come in, but I don't think you'll be seein' that particular group again."

"And if more show up, we'll give 'em the same." Albie grinned.

Ring smiled at the group. "Thanks, everyone. Now, let's get back to the party, shall we?" He lifted his head. "Mr. DJ, how about some dance music?"

People cheered as the opening notes of *Rockin' Robin* reverberated through the room.

Albie stepped forward. "Maddie, would you like to dance?"

She smiled in gratitude. "I'd love too, Albie."

"Can Brutus dance with us?"

"Of course." She turned to Ring. "Excuse me."

"I hope this works, man."

Ring watched her walk away before turning to Dave. "It'd better work. Also, have you heard anything from the guy you put on Anne? It'll probably be a good idea to keep track of her. I don't want her anywhere near Madison."

"I've been busy with this." Dave indicated the room at large as he pulled his cell phone from his pocket. "But I'll check in with him now." He headed back to the kitchen.

Ring walked to the doorway of the parlor. He spotted Madison and Albert Norstock over by the Christmas tree dancing among other people, several of them leaning in to say something to Madison as they danced. The lights from the tree cast a warm glow over Madison's relaxed features as she held the tiny dog and smiled at the old man's dance antics.

"This town loves you, Madison. I love you too and will do whatever it takes to keep you safe."

# Chapter 21

"Good night, Albie." Madison hugged the stooped, thin man. "Merry Christmas."

The old man stepped back. Tears welled in his eyes as his Adam's apple bobbed several times before he spoke. "Thanks, Maddie. It was a good Christmas dinner."

"Oh, wait. I had the caterers pack you some leftovers."

He leaned forward a bit as he pulled his hat on and accepted the bag. "I don't want to insult your fella, but your food is just as good as these fancy folks fixed."

"Are you ready, Albie? Brutus is waiting for you." Chief Lawson stood at the bottom of the steps.

"Yessir. Thank ye for givin' me a ride home."

"You're welcome." Noah Lawson touched the brim of his hat. "Thank you, Miss Madison, for inviting me to dinner, it was a delicious meal again this year."

Maddie smiled at the tall man. "You're welcome, Chief Lawson." She pointed to Ring standing next to her. "But the credit goes to Mr. Stanford. He made the arrangements."

"Thank you." The Texan nodded and touched the brim of his hat again. "Night, folks."

As the car pulled away, Maddie and Ring entered the house. The metallic rattle of chafing pans echoed from the kitchen as the catering staff continued to clean up.

"Thank you again for providing the meal. I would've—"

"I already told you; it was no bother. I don't think you've sat down for more than ten minutes since we got back in town." Ring smiled down at her. "You look exhausted. I think you should head to bed."

"You'll get no protests from me." She yawned and rubbed her abdomen. "The baby's been moving a lot today."

"Are you okay?"

"Yes. Just really tired." Murmurs of conversation drifted out of the kitchen. "What about the caterers?"

"I'll take charge of the caterers."

"You?" Maddie couldn't hide her surprise. "Where's Dave tonight?"

"Sherri invited him to dinner."

"Really? Her parents are here. They always come home from Florida for Christmas. That must've been interesting."

"Hmm, meeting the parents? As if her brother's glares weren't uncomfortable enough."

"Brian? Brian's fine. You just got off on the wrong foot. He's a good guy."

"If you say so." He clasped her hand and pulled Maddie toward the stairway. "Do you need help?"

She shook her head and took several steps up the stairs before she stopped to turn to him. "Dave told me the other night you turned down that movie offer. I'm curious. Why?"

He shrugged. "The timing wasn't right, that's all. Off to bed with you now."

A shadow formed on one of the window curtains for a moment before moving on. "You'll lock up when you leave?"

"I wasn't planning on leaving." He turned to follow her line of sight. "They're here for your protection, Madison."

"Well, since they're here protecting me, I think you should go back to the lake house and get some sleep. I'm not the only one who's been on the go." She shook her head as she climbed the stairs. "Night, Ring."

"Goodnight, Madison. I'll see you tomorrow."

"Hey, man, wake up."

Ring rolled onto his back. It took a moment for him to locate Dave in the dim light of the room. "What time is it?"

"About six-thirty."

"In the morning?" Ring sat up and snapped on the lamp on the nightstand, flipping back the covers. "What's going on?"

Dave smoothed down his mustache. "Well, I just got a call from Sherri. We were supposed to have breakfast this morning, but she canceled."

"Okay. Do you want to get some breakfast?" Ring rose and stretched his large frame. "It's early, but I feel good this—"

"She's at the hospital with Maddie." Dave let out a gust of breath. "They've been there most of the night."

Ring froze. "What's the matter?"

"She's in labor."

"Jesus. Why didn't she call me?"

"Sherri said she was going to call you after the baby was born."

Ring grabbed clothes and headed to the bathroom. "Call the car."

"I already did."

Forty minutes later, they stood at the nurses' station in the birthing pavilion of the hospital. Ring leaned forward and drummed his fingers on the counter. "Hello. I'm looking for Madison O'Neill."

"Madison O'Neill? She's in room..." The nurse looked up and stopped mid-sentence.

"What room?"

"Ahh...room 6."

"Where is it?"

"I'm sorry, Mr. Stanford, but you can't just go in there. You'll have to follow me." She led Dave and Ring to a waiting area where they found Brian Holt slumped in a chair. "Please wait here." With that, she left.

"What's going on?" Dave sat down next to Brian as Ring paced the room.

Brian shook his head and glanced at his watch. "I'm not sure. Sherri hasn't been out in over an hour."

*What is he doing here? Why didn't she call me?* Ring continued to pace until the nurse reappeared in the doorway.

"I'm sorry, you'll have to wait here."

Ring came to stand in front of the woman. "Does she know I'm here? What's going on?"

The nurse nodded. "I told her, but you have to understand, she's very close to delivery. She has a lot going on right now. She needs to focus all her energy on bringing this baby into the world. I'll keep you posted." She turned away and then turned back again. "Can I get your autograph? For my sister?" She pulled a piece of paper and a pen from her pocket. Ring scribbled his name on it and handed it back to her.

"Thanks. There's a small kitchen across the hall if you'd like coffee or juice."

Ring went back to pacing. *What's going on? I thought we were getting close?*

A few minutes later, Dave shoved a paper cup of coffee in his hand. Ring drank without tasting it.

Dave got him another. "Why don't you sit down a minute?"

Ring shook his head.

"Ring?"

He turned. Sherri stood in the doorway, motioning to him. "C'mon."

He followed her down the hall. "What's going on?"

"She's about to deliver."

"Why didn't she call me?"

"Ring, think about it." Sherri rolled her eyes as they hurried down the hall. "You two have never even been together. I can't think of many women that would want this to be the first time a man sees them naked, and no woman alive would want *you*, of all people, to see them like this."

"I don't care about that. I just want to make sure Madison is okay."

"Okay, fine. But my advice, look her in the eyes and tell her that. She's exhausted, and though she hasn't said so, I think she's a little scared."

They pushed through the door.

"Okay, Madison, you're doing great."

Ring glanced at the gowned woman at the foot of the bed for a moment before turning toward Madison. She lay in the bed, her hair a wild cascade on the pillow as she panted.

"Madison, I'm here."

She turned at the sound of his voice, her face shiny and a bit flushed. "Ring."

"I know you're tired, Maddie, but we're almost there." The doctor again. "Are you ready?"

"Yes." Madison closed her eyes a moment as a grimace marred her features before she blew her breath out in a large exhale and pushed. Her efforts ended in a painful cry before she collapsed back on the bed, her breathing ragged. "Sorry, it's hard to talk right now."

He leaned closer. "We don't need to talk. I'm here, I'll be here."

"Ring, you don't need to..." Her sentence ended as a strangled scream through clenched teeth. Maddie collapsed on the bed as tears slipped from the corners of her eyes, her breath coming in huffs. "I'm so tired. I don't know if I can do this."

*I've got to fix this.* "She can't do it. You have to give her something for the pain." Ring raised his voice without looking back, his words clipped.

"There's nothing I can give her at this stage. The baby will be here soon. My suggestion, Mr. Stanford, is you need to help her bring this child into the world."

*Me?*

Madison shifted on the bed as another contraction started.

*Okay.* Ring took a deep breath. *We'll do this together.* He gently held her face in his hands. "Madison, look at me."

She brought her gaze up to meet his.

"You can do this. You're strong and beautiful." He pushed her hair back. "The most beautiful woman I've ever seen." He brought his lips to hers for just a moment. "You can do this."

"Here comes another one. Push, Maddie."

Madison nodded, blew her breath out and gritted her teeth as she bore down for several moments.

"And rest."

*How much more of this can she take?*

Madison lay on the stretcher, her face covered in a fine sheen of perspiration. "You don't have to be—"

Ring laid a finger against her lips. "There's no other place in this world I'd rather be."

"Okay, Madison, one more push, and you'll get to meet your baby. Are you ready?"

Ring held Maddie's gaze. "Are you ready?"

She nodded, gritted her teeth and squeezed Ring's hands as she pushed, the effort lifting her upper body from the bed.

"Good girl. That's my good girl." Ring soothed, not taking his eyes off her. A reedy cry filled the room. They smiled at the sound. "You did it," he whispered.

A few moments later the doctor stepped close to the bed. "There, all dried off. Congratulations. Would you like to meet your daughter?" The doctor laid the baby on Madison's chest.

"A girl? It's a girl?" Maddie placed a hand on the baby's back. Tears slipped down her cheeks in earnest.

*I have a baby girl. I'm a father.* Ring swiped at his own eyes and placed a kiss on Madison's forehead. "She's beautiful."

"She is." Madison sniffed back tears as Ring found her a tissue. "She has your hair and coloring."

He nodded.

Neither spoke for a while as they stared in awe at the perfect little creature until a nurse came in and bustled around, pushing a recliner close to the bed. "How about a little skin-to-skin time with Dad?"

Ring turned to her. "I'm sorry—what are you talking about?"

"Bonding with the baby." The nurse pointed to the chair. "Take your shirt off and have a seat."

He glanced at Madison.

She shrugged and nodded. "It's up to you."

He stripped off his shirt.

The nurse stepped close. "You might want to recline the chair."

He did. The nurse laid the baby on his chest and covered them with a warmed blanket. "Okay, you two, just relax. I'm going to help Mom freshen up." She pulled the privacy curtain around Maddie's bed.

Ring studied the tiny red hand, fingers flat against the dark skin of his chest. *Look at you. So beautiful.* The baby moved. Ring stiffened and opened his mouth to call the nurse until he glanced down. Beneath a mass of black hair, two dark eyes studied him intently. "Hello, beautiful," he whispered with a smile as tears welled again. *I promise I'll be there for you. Always.* In that moment, Ring Stanford realized he was truly in love, maybe for the first time in his life.

# Chapter 22

Madison set a plate of cookies on the coffee table and glanced around the room. *Everything seems to be in its place. The T.V., it doesn't need to be on.* Ring had been watching it earlier as he held the baby. She reached for the remote only to pause.

"*In entertainment news, it's the second time actress Anne Reese Miller's captured headlines recently. Earlier this week, in a written statement, she apologized to all concerned for accusing a Vermont woman of stealing her baby. She blamed the episode—as she referred to the press conference, on stress, her rocky estrangement from husband, Ring Stanford, and grief over ending a brief relationship with famed director, Arthur Von Timber. Then, just this morning, in a taped interview for Hollywood View, she announced she's been cast in Cameron Scott's new movie. When asked about her future project and reconciliation with her husband, Ring Stanford, Ms. Miller smiled and said time will tell. Mr. Stanford was unavailable for comment. So—there you have it, folks. Time will tell. This is Dave Signet and Just Another Day in Hollywood.*"

Madison clicked the remote and stared at the blank screen a moment. *What a piece of work, but at least the security guards are gone.* She moved to the sofa where the baby slept on a blanket. *She's so tiny.*

The phone rang and Maddie grabbed it. "Hello?"

"Hi. How are you feeling?"

She sighed "I'm fine, Ring." *He's referring to this morning.* Maddie had broken down and cried when she burnt some toast. "I'm fine now, really. I told you, I think it was a touch of the baby blues. It'll get better."

"I googled it. Postpartum depression. You should get some rest, it'll help."

"I will."

"How is she?"

She smiled at Ring's question. "She's sleeping."

"Then why don't you get some rest too while the house is quiet?"

Ever since Ring brought Maddie and the baby home from the hospital two days ago there'd been a steady stream of visitors. "I will, but Sherri's coming over with a dish her mother made at some point." Maddie cleared her throat. "Is your mother there yet?"

"Yes. She landed about half an hour ago. Actually, we're in the car and headed back. She can't wait to meet you."

Maddie remained silent.

"Madison?"

"Yes. Yes. I can't explain it, but I feel anxious, or scared or something...I don't know."

"Why? Is something going on?"

"No. No. It's me. I feel edgy. That's the only way I can explain it."

"I think it's all part of this postpartum thing. Try to relax, and we'll be there before you know it. Okay?"

She sighed again. "Okay."

A knock sounded on the front door.

"Oh, that must be Sherri. I have to go."

"We'll see you in a few minutes."

"Yes, see you soon." Madison disconnected, set the phone back in its cradle and opened the door. "Hi, Sherri, thanks—"

It wasn't Sherri. Despite the dark glasses she wore, Madison recognized Anne Reese Miller. Out of instinct she closed the portal a bit and blocked the opening. "Yes?"

The woman slid the glasses down her nose and peered over them. "Wow. You're Madison O'Neill?"

Madison gripped the edge of the door and resisted the urge to smooth her hair. She hadn't bothered with any makeup. "Yes."

"You don't look much like your picture." The woman pulled off her glasses and looked Maddie up and down with a shake of her head. "Really, Ring?" She muttered.

"I beg your pardon?" Tears welled as Madison tightened her grip on the wood. *Don't let her get to you.*

"Was he high when you two got together? He says he's not using, but I find that hard to believe. You're not his type at all."

A flash of irritation surged through Maddie's gut. "What do you want?"

"Well, darling, I was just passing through town." The woman's smile was ingratiating and well rehearsed.

"No, you weren't."

"No, you're right. I came to see you." Anne's gaze narrowed. "Look, I want to make sure you have no illusions about a future with Ring. You may have gotten him between your legs once, and that baby may even be his, which I doubt, but he's my husband, and I have no plans to give him a divorce."

Maddie bit down on her lower lip to keep from responding to the crass comments.

"If there's one thing I know about Ring Stanford—he starts things, but he's not a finisher. Sooner or later, he'll get tired of hanging out here in Green Acres and come back home." Anne studied her manicured nails a moment. "And I'll be waiting." She smiled again, her brilliant red lipstick emphasizing perfect white teeth before giving Madison another head to toe look. "And from the looks of you, it should take no time at all. Ta. Ta." She turned away with a swing of her dark hair only to turn back. "Of course, he may want to keep the child." She shrugged. "And I may even let him. It'll be easy enough—we have very good lawyers."

Her smug smile was short lived as Maddie ripped open the door and advanced on her. "If you come near my baby, I'll make you rue the day you were born."

Despite her stilettos, Anne was already halfway down the walkway when the small wrought iron table Maddie tossed landed at her heels, followed by one of the matching chairs.

"You crazy bitch!"

"You'll see just how crazy I am if you ever come back here," Madison shouted as tears streamed down her face. She started down the porch steps with the last chair only to have Anne climb into the back of a waiting limo and speed away. She slumped to the stairs. *What's wrong with me?*

Several minutes passed as Maddie's sobs diminished to loud sniffles. It was then she heard the baby crying. The chair clattered down the steps as she released it and hurried inside to scoop up the infant. "Shh. Shh." She walked around the living room gently rocking the baby. *What have I gotten myself into with these people?* She was still pacing when Ring came through the open front door.

"Madison? What's going on? Are you okay?"

She shook her head and continued to move.

He stepped closer and caught her by the arm to stop her. "What's wrong?"

Tears threatened again and Maddie swallowed, but remained silent.

"Madison, talk to me. Is the baby okay?"

She nodded. "Your wife was here."

"What? Son of a bitch!" He pulled out his phone and punched a number. "Dave, what are we paying these people for? Anne showed up here. I want security back—now."

Madison laid a hand on his arm. "No."

"Hold on a second, Dave. Madison, you have to. It's for your protection and the baby's."

"No. This isn't going to work."

"Dave, I'll call you back in a minute." Ring disconnected the phone. "It will work. I promise she won't get anywhere near you again."

"Hello? Ring?" A voice sounded from outside the house.

"Damn it. My mother. I forgot about her when I saw the door open. Can we talk about this later?"

Maddie nodded.

"Thank you." He turned away. "I'm sorry, Mom, right here. Come in." He led a tall, thin, well dressed woman with soft gray hair into the living room. "Madison, this is my mother Lillian Stanford. Mom, this is Madison O'Neill."

"Hello, dear."

The woman's genuine smile put Madison more at ease and she returned the smile. "Hi, it's nice to meet you. Please have a seat. Would you like some tea or coffee?"

Lillian settled on the sofa. "Tea would be wonderful. But first, don't you two have someone else to introduce me to?"

"Of course." Madison moved closer to Ring. "Why don't you do it?" Her words were soft. "I'll make tea."

"Really?" His furrowed brow smoothed as Maddie laid the baby in his arms. "Thank you," he mouthed before sitting on the couch next to his mother. "Would you like to hold her?"

"Yes. Very much." Lillian cradled the infant in her arms and studied her sleeping face.

"Mom, this is Liliana O'Neill-Stanford." His words held a hint of pride. "After you and Madison's mother, Anna."

"That's a lovely name. She looks a lot like you did when you were born." She placed a tender kiss on the baby's head. "Hello, my beautiful Liliana. You are so precious." Tears sparkled in the woman's eyes as she turned to Ring. "You did good, son."

"Thanks. She's the best thing that's ever come into my life." He smiled and looked up at Madison. "She and her mother."

Maddie blushed. "I'll get the tea." A few minutes later, she returned to sit in the chair on the other side of the coffee table.

"And how are you feeling, Madison?"

"I'm fine, Mrs. Stanford."

"Please call me Lil, everyone does." The woman continued to cuddle the baby. "There must've been quite a wind storm to blow all that furniture off the porch."

*I could just agree.* "No, no wind."

"Really?"

"Mrs. Stan—Lil." Madison cleared her throat. "As much as it pains me to admit it, that's my fault. I lost my temper."

The woman's eyebrows raised a bit. "Well, everyone loses their temper once in a while, dear. You must've had a good reason."

"No, not—"

"Anne was here," Ring supplied.

A warm flush started up Madison's neck. *She's going to think I'm crazy.*

Lillian gave a snort. "Well, that explains a lot. Did she wreck your porch?" She turned to Ring. "When will you be done with that woman? She's poison."

"I'm working on—"

"She didn't touch them. It was me." Maddie's cheeks burned. "I threw them at her."

"Well, good enough. If I know that she-cat, and I do, she was trying to cause trouble."

"Maybe, but I didn't have to sink to that level."

"Ring, could you hold Liliana, please?" Lillian handed the baby over and scooted forward a bit on the couch to reach for her tea. "Don't be so hard on yourself." She took a sip from the cup. "Anne deserved it, I'm sure."

"Maybe, but this isn't about who she is—it's about who I am." Maddie laid a hand flat against her chest. "I don't shout at people—and I've never thrown anything at anyone in my life."

"Well, I can't think of a better target for your first try." A slight smile touched Lillian's lips behind the cup. "Did you hit her?"

"No, thank goodness." Madison shook her head. "I can't keep going on like this. It has to end."

"It'll work out," Ring insisted.

"No, it won't. I just want a normal life."

"This is normal."

"Who're you trying to kid, Ring? Limos, fan mobs, security details? That's not normal."

"I know it can be a bit overwhelming, but, dear, you must've known your life would change a bit when you became romantically involved with Ring."

"Lillian, has Ring told you the circumstances around my pregnancy?"

The woman nodded.

"Then you know we weren't romantically involved." Madison sighed and ran a hand through her hair. "We don't exactly travel in the same circles. In fact, if it wasn't for Liliana, we would've never met."

"You don't know that," Ring spoke up.

"I do; and so do you—if you were being honest with yourself."

"I disagree." He shook his head.

"You know, there are those that believe everything happens just the way it's supposed to. I prefer to believe that and the fact that it led to this sweet baby." Lillian smiled at Madison. "And that you and my son were meant to meet."

"You may be right, but regardless, I just want peace and quiet." Madison directed her next comment to Ring. "She made it very clear she has no intention of giving you a divorce."

"And you threw furniture at her to protect my honor?" Ring joked.

"No...when she threatened to take the baby."

The smile dropped from Ring's face. "That's not going to happen." He pulled out his phone. "Get them back here—now."

Maddie shook her head as silent tears slid down her cheeks. "I've told you all along this wasn't going to work."

"You're tired. You need some rest," Ring cajoled. "C'mon."

"The baby will need to be fed and changed."

"There's a bottle in the fridge, right? And don't forget, I've personally changed a few diapers."

"You're kidding?" Lillian laughed. "This I've got to see. Don't worry, Madison, I'll help him look after her. You'll feel so much better after a couple of hours of sleep."

Ring walked with her to the stairs.

"What about dinner? I wanted to make something nice for your mother."

"I'll take care of it."

"More catering?"

"I don't know, but we'll handle it." He leaned forward and placed a gentle kiss against her lips. "Get some rest."

Madison climbed the stairs, kicked off her shoes and slipped beneath the covers.

# Chapter 23

Ring laid napkins and silverware on the kitchen table.

"I think it's done." Sherri grabbed a couple of pot holders and opened the oven door. "My mother put it together because she knows Maddie loves lasagna." Sherri placed the pan on the island.

"It smells great." Ring set out a stack of plates before he retrieved glasses from the cupboard to add to the place settings.

"Am I seeing this right? You're setting a table?"

Ring turned at his mother's voice. "Can you believe it? Me?"

"No, actually I can't. Diaper changes, feedings and now this...I'd say this life agrees with you."

"I've been thinking the same thing lately—a lot." He smiled at his mother's raised eyebrows. "I'm serious."

She nodded. "Okay. You don't see me disagreeing."

Ring returned her nod. "Is she asleep?"

Lillian smiled. "Like a little angel. What do you need help with?"

"You can get the salad out of the fridge. I'm warming the garlic bread." Sherri peeked in the oven again. "Almost done. Ring, can you grab one of those wicker bread baskets? Dave should be here any minute." She took a sip of wine. "Should we wake up Maddie to eat dinner?"

Ring glanced at his watch and shook his head. "She's been asleep since about 1:00, but I think she needs sleep more than food at this point."

A knock sounded at the front door and Ring went to answer it. Dave Martinez stood on the other side, but he wasn't alone. Albie Norstock stood beside him shuffling from foot to foot.

"Hey, Dave." Ring glanced at the man next to his manager. "Hi, Albie. How are you doing?"

"Fine." The man continued to shift.

"Albie here," Dave rested a hand on the thin man's shoulder, "has been wondering how Madison's doing. He knows she needs her rest, so he didn't want to disturb her, but he was hoping he'd catch someone to ask." The trace of a smile was not lost despite the Hispanic man's bushy mustache.

"Yessir, that's it." Albie pulled off his hat. His cheeks looked freshly scrubbed and his thinning hair had been slicked back. "I thought these security people left, but I ain't been able to get near the place tonight—until I saw this fella here and he recognized me. How's she doin'?"

Ring nodded. "She's recuperating, Albie. Where's Brutus?"

Albie jerked a thumb to his right. "I left him at home. I wasn't sure how long I'd have to wait outside, and I didn't want him to get cold."

"Well, why don't you come in? Madison's sleeping right now, but she may be up soon." Ring closed the door after the two men. "Would you like to meet the baby?"

Albie's nod was eager.

Ring led him to a small bassinet in the living room. The soft lamplight nearby illuminated the sleeping newborn, her arms stretched above her head. "This is Liliana."

The old man studied the baby with a rapt expression on his grizzled face. "She's beautiful," he whispered after several moments. "The most beautiful thing I've ever seen."

"I think so too." Ring smiled and stepped away, motioning Albie to follow. "Since you're here, do you have dinner plans?"

"Dinner plans? Me? Naw. I was going to have a can of pork and beans later."

"Why don't you stay and eat with us?"

"Really?" The old man sniffed the air. "That smells like Esther Holt's lasagna." Sherri set the bread basket on the table. "I knew it." He tucked his hat in his pocket and shrugged off his baggy overcoat. "Well, I'm not one to turn my nose up at good food."

"Great." They joined the others in the kitchen. "Albie, this is my mother Lillian. Mom, this is Albie, a family friend of Madison's."

Lillian held out her hand.

"Albert Norstock." Instead of shaking it, the man placed a light kiss on the back of her hand. "At your service, ma'am."

A spot of color formed on each of Lillian's cheeks as she smiled at the man. "It's my pleasure to meet you, Albert."

*Are they flirting with each other?* Ring shook his head to dismiss the thought. *It can't be.* "Shall we?"

Albie and Lillian each sat at an end of the table. Dave and Sherri sat on one side, while Ring sat on the other side. Food was consumed while Albie Norstock spun tales to keep them all entertained.

Ring found himself laughing along with the others at the old man's stories. He glanced around the group. Everyone was smiling and relaxed. He leaned back in his chair as realization struck. *This is what family is supposed to feel like. This is the good life.* The thought generated a warmth deep inside of Ring's gut. He looked up to find Madison standing in the doorway, her hair disheveled and sleep lingering on her features. *She's so beautiful. I want this life with her.*

"Hi, everyone." She yawned behind a hand. "Sorry, I slept so long."

Ring got up and ushered her to the table. "That's fine. You needed the sleep. Look who came to visit."

Maddie's eyes lit up and a smile touched her lips. "Albie. It's good to see you." She bent down to hug him. "I was wondering where you were."

"I was waiting for you to feel better."

"I'm getting there. I think that nap did wonders." She glanced at his dinner plate. "Is that Mrs. Holt's lasagna?"

Sherri nodded. "She made it for you. Why don't you sit down, and I'll get you some?"

Madison slid into the empty seat next to Ring. "Where's Liliana?"

"Sleeping," Lillian reassured her. "She's such a darling."

Sherri put a plate in front of Maddie.

"She's a looker, Maddie." Albie grinned. "Just like the rest of the O'Neill family."

Ring cleared his throat and gave the man a mock frown.

"Well, you're okay lookin' too." The old man shrugged and pointed a fork at Ring. "But nowhere near the looker Maddie is."

Everyone at the table burst out laughing.

"You're right, of course. She is a looker." Ring turned to Madison with a smile and gave her a quick kiss.

Maddie blushed.

No one else seemed to notice. Ring slipped his hand into hers under the table, intertwining their fingers. Maddie didn't pull her hand away.

*This is so right. I want a life with this woman.* What about Anne? *Face it, she's not going to give you a divorce. What are we going to do?*

Later, when everyone else left, Ring opted to stay a while longer. They sat on the sofa in front of the fireplace, Madison holding a sleeping Liliana.

Ring lightly traced a finger down the baby's cheek. "I love you," he whispered. He turned his dark gaze to Madison. "I love you too."

She maintained eye contact but remained silent for several moments. "I know you think you do, but having a baby can be an emotional experience for all involved. You might be confusing that with love."

He shook his head. "I'm not. I loved you long before Liliana was born. You. I love you."

"But you know it won't work—"

"It will work out. It already has. The reporters have moved on to someone else. We're old news. We had a family dinner tonight without one paparazzi present. It'll work." He clasped her free hand. "Do you love me?"

She swallowed before speaking in a low voice. "Yes. I didn't want to, but I do. It won't—"

He leaned forward and gave her a tender kiss. "It will. What do I have to do to convince you of that? Do you want me to stop acting?"

"What?"

"I'll stop. If that's what you want."

"And do what?"

He shrugged. "I don't know—work in a hardware store?"

She raised an eyebrow. "Do you know anything about hardware?"

"No. The only thing I know is we love each other, and I want to make a life with you and our baby." He hesitated a moment. "There's one thing."

"What's that?"

"I need to get this whole thing with Anne settled."

"She's not going to divorce you. She said so today."

"One way or another—if I have to give her every last dime, I'm not staying married to her."

"Well, then, you really might have to go to work in the hardware store."

He kissed the top of the baby's head. "I don't think I'd care, if I got to come home to you and Liliana every day."

"I think not. You like the finer things in life too much." Maddie's smile was sad. "So, what are you going to do?"

"I'm not sure. Dave and I have been talking. I may need to go back for a few days. My mother can come and stay with you while I'm gone."

"She doesn't have to do that."

"Are you kidding?" Ring grinned. "She's salivating at the chance."

Maddie nodded. "When are you leaving?"

"Probably tomorrow. The sooner we get this over, the better." He rose. "C'mon. I'll tuck you and Liliana in." He lifted the baby out of Maddie's arms and clasped her hand as they climbed the stairs.

# Chapter 24

Ring glanced again at the lights of downtown L.A. below before leaving the pool area to step into the austere atmosphere of the dining room. A table for sixteen dominated the space. His footsteps echoed as he continued through the sparsely furnished house to pass a set of open marble stairs leading to the next floor. He hadn't bothered to use one of the seven bedrooms above. Instead, he'd slept on the covered patio set up as an outdoor bedroom near the pool.

*What did I ever see in this place?* Everything was white. Every piece of furniture, the marble floors and walls, even the never-driven Lamborghini and Mercedes parked in the garage were white. Ring shook his head. *I must've been high.* He took a drink from the glass in his hand. *What's taking Dave so long?*

He wandered down the stairs to the lower level. *Maybe a movie?* Not only was there a home theater down here, but a bowling alley, night club, salon and gym. Not to mention the other facilities in outlying buildings. *I can't blame this house on Anne.* He'd bought it before they met. Ring knew the answer. He'd been caught up in the status of living on Billionaire's Row in Beverly

Hills. *How could I have thought this is what mattered?* After Madison's colorful house with its homemade afghans, this place felt cold and stark. *This is not a home.* He took another drink.

The faint sound of a buzzer echoed from above. Ring hurried back up the stairs. Much to Dave's dismay, upon arrival, he'd let the staff go, each with a generous severance.

*Where's that coming from?* He followed the sound down a short hallway to several doors. The first door he opened was an empty closet. As soon as he opened the next door, the buzz got louder. *What the hell?* Ring left the door open and stepped into the cramped space. A chair and a small table filled the area. The table held a video monitor and panel box with numerous buttons and switches.

On the screen, Dave sat outside the gate in an Escalade drumming his fingers on the steering wheel. "C'mon, Ring, I forgot the remote. What's takin' so long? I've been here ten minutes."

*Christ, someone actually sat in here?* Ring studied the control panel until he found a switch labeled main gate. He flipped it and the gate began to move.

"It's about time," Dave muttered, creeping forward. Ring flipped the switch back and the huge SUV barely squeaked through before the gate closed on it.

A few minutes later, Ring swung the door open at Dave's knock.

"Very funny, man. Can you at least find someone who knows how to run the gate?" Dave stepped through the door. "I found a delivery guy trying to figure out how to get in." He held out a square flat box. "You actually ordered a pizza—yourself?"

"Well, it took a few minutes, but I felt like a pizza."

"You're kidding? You let a world class chef go to order pizza?"

Ring shrugged, took the box from him and headed toward the kitchen.

"What're you doing now?"

"I'm hungry. I'm getting some plates and a beer. You want one?" It took several minutes of searching for dishes to locate them. They sat at the table chewing on the cold pizza. "Who knew we had a separate dish room? I've never even been in this kitchen." Ring took another bite. "Where've you been?"

"Where've I been?" Dave shook his head. "Everywhere. In case you've forgotten, we've been away for a while. I needed to take care of business."

"I know. I know. Did you get everything done?"

"Most of it. I arranged for the car and driver your mother wanted while she's in Northam. Maddie refused the chef you sent, but agreed to a grocery delivery. As Sherri put it, she and your mother have been cooking up a storm together. Sherri's been over there for dinner twice this week." Dave hesitated a moment. "Guess who else has been there every night?"

Ring's eyes narrowed a bit. "Brian Holt?"

"Naw, man." Dave shook his head. "Albie."

"You're kidding?"

"Nope."

"Well, whadda you know?" Ring took a sip of beer.

"Ah, there's something else. It seems your mother has looked at several houses this week."

"To buy?"

Dave nodded.

"Well, that's good, right? You can't blame her for wanting to be near her grandchild?"

"Not at all." Dave took a drink of his beer. "It seems she's asked Albie to go with her to look."

That brought raised eyebrows from Ring. "Hmm, I wonder what that's about?"

"No idea, man."

"Well, the sooner we get back there, the sooner we'll know. Did you hear from the guy watching Anne—who'd you hire, by the way?"

"Joe Dickson. He's good. I got a phone call from him last night. He said he might be onto something and he'd let me know."

"Did he tell you what it was?"

"No, but he'll call."

"I hope so. I'm tired of being here."

"Ring, we've only been back a week."

"That's a week too long. I want to get back to Northam."

Dave cleared his throat. "Ahh, this might not be the best time to mention it, but you've only got a little while longer before you're supposed to go back to work."

Ring got up and grabbed more beer from the fridge, setting one down in front of Dave before opening the one he held. "I know." He took a swallow and studied the side of the can. "I'd rather take a break and spend time with Madison and Liliana. Maybe the house on Antigua?"

"Ring you've got—"

"I know, obligations." Ring sighed. "As soon as—"

Dave's phone rang. "Joe Dickson." He pushed a button. "Hi, Joe. How's it goin'?" He listened for a moment. "What? Here?

Now?" He laid the phone against his chest to block the speaker. "He's at the gate. He says he has somebody we should talk to."

"Who?"

Dave lifted the phone. "Who? Malcolm Bridgely? Never heard of him. Ring?"

"I don't know him."

David listened a moment more. "Okay. Okay. He says we need to hear this."

"Fine. I'll open the gate." Ring came back just as Dave admitted the two men.

Joe Dickson, bald and built, towered over the skinny man next to him. "This is Malcolm."

Ring watched the little man shift from foot to foot as he ran a shaking hand through a poorly done comb over.

"I'm Ring Stanford." He stepped closer.

The man swallowed and took a step back. His Adam's apple moved up and down like a fishing bobber riding the waves. "I know who you are."

"Great." Ring patted the man's shoulder. "Would you like a beer?" He glanced at his manager with a slight lift of his head. Dave headed to the kitchen. "Do you want one, Joe?"

"Not while I'm working."

Dave handed the beer to the nervous man, who cracked it open and poured a good share down his throat in one swallow before looking at the can. "This is good stuff." Malcolm's belch was loud in the quiet of the room. "Real good stuff." He swallowed the remains of the can.

"Dave."

Another beer was offered to Malcolm. His drink wasn't quite as big this time and his burp not as loud, but his shoulders visibly relaxed.

"So, Mr. Bridgely, you had something to tell us?"

"I do. And I'll take another one of these beers if you got it." The man grinned and glanced around the entryway. "Nice place you got here. Real nice." He took another pull off the can. "How much is this information worth to you?"

"You're *loco* if you—"

Ring laid a hand on his manager's arm. "Dave, why don't you get Malcolm another beer?"

Dave shook his head. "Sure."

Ring smiled at Bridgely. "How can I gauge what this information's worth if I don't know what it is?"

"True." The man nodded, took another swig and wiped his mouth off on his sleeve. "Okay. I just got out of Lancaster."

"Lancaster? What's that?"

"California State Prison. In Lancaster County," Joe Dickson supplied.

"For what?"

The man raised his bony shoulders. "Does it matter?"

Ring remained silent.

"It weren't murder or nothin'. Drugs—sellin' drugs. Five years this time." Malcolm shook his head and finished off the beer. "Last year, they put this guy in my cell. Benson Furmont. He was a real bastard and made my life hell to begin with—until I figured out how to please him." The man's face flushed a deep red. "If you know what I mean." His shoulders rose and fell again. "You gotta do what you gotta do to survive. Ya know what I mean?"

Ring nodded.

The man shook the empty can.

"Dave will be right back. You were saying?"

"Oh, yeah. Anyway, one night after we...you know—we were layin' there, talkin'. And he starts tellin' me about jobs he's done. He had a very interestin' line of work."

"Malcolm, what's this got to do with me?" Ring tipped his head to the side to flex the muscles at the back of his neck.

"I'm gettin' to that part." Malcolm took the fresh beer Dave offered and shoved the empty can into his hand.

"Continue." Ring crossed his arms and waited as the man took another drink.

"What am I, the butler now?" Dave muttered as he turned away, only to stop a few seconds later at Malcolm's next words.

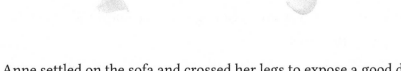

Anne settled on the sofa and crossed her legs to expose a good deal of thigh before accepting the drink from Ring. "Thank you, darling. How long have you been back?"

"A couple of weeks."

"And you didn't call me before now? Shame on you." She took a sip from the squat glass. "Ahh, that's perfect. Aren't you having one?"

Ring lifted the beer in his hand.

"Beer? Really? And right out of the can?"

He shrugged.

"Suit yourself. Did you bring your mistress back with you?"

He shook his head.

"It's good to see you've come to your senses." Anne smiled as she looked around. "I always loved this place. So cool. Such clean lines." When Ring didn't respond, she continued on. "So, what's so urgent I had to come over here today? I don't know if you've heard, but I got a part in the new Cameron Scott movie—it's perfect for me. I'm in the middle of packing. Filming starts in Ireland next week."

"I'm glad to hear it."

She studied the liquid in her glass for a few moments. "Ring, now that you're back, we can work this out. We were good together." She scooted forward on the sofa. "We can be good again. Don't give up on us, baby." She reached out a hand and rested it on the inside of his thigh.

Ring took a step back.

She narrowed her gaze. "Look, if this has anything to do with your supposed baby mama, you might as well know right now, I'm not signing the papers."

"This has nothing to do with Madison...this is between you and me."

"Well, at least you can see this is about us. I'm glad you're finally home." Anne set her glass down and rose to slide her arms along Ring's sides and pull him closer. "It'll be better this time, baby, I promise." She rubbed up against him. "Trust me."

"Trust you? You cheated on me. Trust has to be earned."

She sighed. "Fine. What can I do to earn your trust?"

Ring didn't move. "Do you know Malcolm Bridgely?"

"Who?" She whispered as her hands slid down his torso.

"Malcolm Bridgely?"

"Never heard of him." Her hands stopped at his belt.

"He knows about you."

She continued to work the buckle in an attempt to open it as she shrugged. "Lots of people know me. I have thousands of fans—you know that, darling."

"It seems you two have a mutual friend. Benson Furmont."

Her hands slowed. "I have no idea who you're talking about."

"I think you do."

Anne stepped back. "I told you. I don't know who these people are, Ring. What's important right now is our relationship. You know you still love me—I can tell just by looking at your face. And I love you." She reached for him again. "We can make this work."

Ring put a hand out to stop her. "You love me?"

"Of course I do. I'm here, aren't I? We can make this work. If you want a baby, I'll have a baby. Anything." Her words held a note of desperation.

"Anything?"

"Yes, yes. Anything."

"We need to be honest with each other. That's the only way I'll be able to trust you again."

"Yes, of course. Whatever you want." She blinked several times forcing a single tear down her cheek.

"Who are Malcolm Bridgely and Benson Furmont?"

"I told you already, I don't know. Ring—"

"This won't work." He turned away.

"Wait." She swallowed and held up a hand. "First of all, I want you to know, I was confused and high. I didn't know what I was doing."

He turned back.

Anne picked up her glass and drained it. "I have no idea who Malcolm—whatever his name was, is." She paced to the glass wall and back and stood silent for several moments before exhaling a large gust of breath. "I hired Benson Furmont."

"To do what?"

She tapped her fingers on the back of the couch. "A job for me."

"What job?"

"Ring, please—it's in the past. I'm sorry. I didn't know what I was doing. Stop," she shouted at his retreating back.

He did an about face and came to stand within a foot of her. "What job did he do for you?"

"I, ahh, wanted him to take someone out."

"Why?"

"I wanted—needed more money. I was used to a certain life style—" A sob caught in her throat. "And I thought..." Anne hung her head.

"Look at me."

She brought her gaze up to meet his.

"What'd you do, Anne?" He moved his lips to within an inch of hers, his tone seductive, "Trust, remember?"

"Yes, trust." She stood transfixed and nodded. "Boston. He's the one that shot you in Boston." She leaned in, closing the gap between them. "There, now you know. I'm sorry I did it," she whispered.

Ring pulled back and shook his head. "No, you're only sorry I lived. We were separated, but as my wife you would've gotten everything."

"I said I'm sorry, and I'm thankful you made it. Can we move on now?" Though she tried to hide it, a definite hint of annoyance laced her question.

"Really? Sorry is supposed to cut it?"

Anne frowned. "What do you mean?"

"You do realize that's a crime?"

"Yes, but it's different now. I want you back." She tried to put her arms around him.

*What did I ever see in this woman?* Ring held up hands to ward her off. "I don't want you."

"What're you talking about? You love me."

"You belong in jail."

"Don't be silly. It was a misunderstanding. I'm not going to jail." A look of defiance settled on her features. "Besides, you'll have to prove it—it's your word against mine."

Footsteps sounded in the hallway.

"Actually, it's not. It's your words."

Several men in dark suits entered the room. One of them approached Anne with a set of handcuffs. "Anne Reese Miller, you're under arrest for conspiracy to commit murder and attempted murder."

"What? This can't be happening." She tried to pull away from the detective only to end up with her hands manacled behind her back. "You set me up? How could you do this? You love me."

"Maybe once, a long time ago. But now, this just proves I'm a better actor than you are." Ring shook his head as the policemen led her away.

# Chapter 25

*Eleven months later...*

Ring and Dave exited the jet, hustled through the terminal and stepped outside where a black limo waited at the curb. A man climbed out from behind the steering wheel and loaded their suitcases in the trunk.

"Hi, Harold, how's everything?"

The man closed the trunk lid. "Good and yourself, Mr. Stanford?"

"Glad to be home."

The driver opened the rear door.

"Why aren't you driving the Navigator?"

The man smiled. "I got permission to bring the limo, considering it's a special occasion."

Ring nodded. "Our tux?"

"In the back, sir, per your instructions."

"Great." Ring glanced at his watch. "We're going to be late. We'll have to change in the car."

All three men climbed in the vehicle, and a few minutes later merged with traffic on the highway. Ring glanced out the window. "Is there more traffic than usual?"

Dave looked up from his phone a moment, shrugged and dropped his eyes again.

Ring kicked off his shoes. "Are you changing?"

"In just a minute. Damn."

Ring paused in unbuttoning his shirt. "What's wrong?"

"Well, I know you like the script for the Santos sequel, but Hanson just upped his offer for that western. The problem is their shooting schedules overlap. Have you looked at that script yet?"

"Not yet. I plan on reading through it sometime in the next couple of weeks."

"Good. Man, ever since you took home Oscar, the offers have been pouring in. What do you think about a mini-series?"

Ring shook his head. "Not interested."

"But, Ring, it'd be great for your—"

"No. I told you, no more than three projects a year, and lately, that feels like too many." Ring pulled off his shirt.

"Okay. Okay. But Santos wants a meeting in a few weeks."

"Maybe, I'll have to check schedules."

Dave continued to scroll through his phone for awhile before he spoke again. "Ring."

"What?"

"Holy crap."

"What?"

"They sentenced Anne."

Ring testified at her trial, but after much discussion and thought had also asked the court for leniency since Anne had a drug problem. That created quite a stir in the papers, but Ring offered no comment to the press. *As someone reminded me, it was the right thing to do because it's about who I am, not who she is.*

Benson Furmont's trial had been earlier in the year. He was sentenced to life without parole. It hadn't fazed him in the least. He was already serving consecutive life sentences and for his corroborating testimony against Anne, he was being moved to better facilities.

Dave gave a low whistle. "The judge made a public statement. He was inclined to give her life, but in light of your testimony, he sentenced her to fifty years. She'll be eligible for parole in twenty."

Ring shook his head. "That's a lot of years."

"It is, but remember, man, she tried to end you and came pretty close to success."

"I know."

"Do you have a T.V. in the house these days?"

Ring shook his head. "Nope. And that's the way I want to keep it."

"It's probably just as well." Dave tucked his phone away. "Okay. Are you ready for this?"

Ring grinned and nodded. "You should change." He slid forward and tucked the back of the white ruffled shirt he wore into the waist band of black tuxedo pants. "It's not as easy as it sounds." He glanced at his watch again. "Harold, can you step on it a little bit? We still have to stop at the house before we go to the church."

The rest of the ride was spent working their way into the tuxedos.

Ring finished his bow tie as the car pulled into the drive. He looked toward the house in anticipation. There, on the walkway, was his beautiful little girl, in a ruffly pink dress, clinging to her mother's hand.

He bolted from the car. "Hello, sweetheart."

The baby responded to his grin with a big smile of her own, showing two top and two bottom teeth.

Madison put up her hand. "Stop. Wait right there."

Ring halted three feet from them.

She bent down next to the baby. "Are you ready? Let's show him." She loosened the baby's grip on her fingers. "Ring, hold out your hands. Okay, Liliana. Go to Daddy."

The baby teetered for a moment before taking one step, followed by another.

"C'mon, baby girl. Come to Daddy," Ring encouraged, his face lit with wonder.

Liliana smiled and took several more steps before falling into his arms.

He scooped up the baby and gave her a kiss and a squeeze. "She's walking?"

Maddie nodded as she joined them. "Just this week."

"You look beautiful." He leaned in and kissed Maddie. "I've missed you."

"I've missed you too." Madison reached up to straighten his tie. "You look very handsome yourself, sir. How was the trip home?"

"Long. Boring."

"Well, this is going to be a long day. I hope you got some rest on the plane."

"A little." Ring grinned. "It's going to be a great day. Combining the reception and the Harvest Ball was a brilliant idea. I'm glad the committee agreed."

"Of course they did. Why wouldn't they?" Madison's smile was almost a smirk. "You're paying for the whole thing and donating cash to boot? What's not to like?"

"Absolutely nothing. The sun is shining, it's a beautiful fall day, and I'm with my ladies—both of who look very fetching, by the way. Nice job on the dresses."

Madison blushed with pleasure. "Thank you. I wanted to keep it simple."

He laid a gentle hand along the back of Madison's neck to pull her closer. "There's nothing simple about you." His lips touched hers in a lingering kiss. "You're so beautiful. I love you so much, sometimes it's a physical hurt, worse than any addiction, but one I'm not willing to give up," he whispered against her lips.

"Hey, you guys; how do I look?" Dave climbed out of the limo and came to stand next to Ring. He leaned close to Liliana. "Hello, pretty baby. Is Aunt Sherri here?" She reached for his mustache. Dave backed up. "Oh, no you don't, not again. Uncle Dave is wise to your moves." He reached out to grasp her tiny fingers and give them a kiss.

"Sherri went home to finish packing a while ago. She should be back any minute," Maddie supplied. "Where are you guys flying this time?"

"L.A. for a few days. I want to show her some of the sights."

"She's very excited." Maddie gave Dave an inquisitive look. "You are coming to the Ball tonight?"

The swarthy man nodded and smoothed down his mustache. "It seems like the appropriate place to ask Sherri a question and offer her this." He pulled a small box from his pocket and opened it. A ring set with a huge diamond sparkled in the sunlight.

"Oh, Dave, congratulations." Maddie hugged him. "Have you figured out where you guys are going to live?"

"I have no idea." He shrugged. "And, honestly, I don't care. I love that woman so much, it's drivin' me crazy. You and Ring have convinced me it can work."

A car horn sounded and Sherri pulled her low slung Hyundai into the driveway next to the limo. A minute later, she threw her arms around Dave and kissed him soundly before pulling back. "Hi there. Did you miss me?"

He kept an arm around her waist. "Every day."

Sherri grinned. "Me too."

A car zoomed by, laying on the horn.

"They're headed to the church. We'd better get going." Sherri pulled Dave toward the limo.

"What are they going to do, start without us?" Ring laughed as he and Maddie climbed in too and buckled Liliana into her car seat.

Madison stood at the back of the church holding a bouquet of pale pink roses. She could see Ring standing at the front with the others.

Dave leaned in and spoke to him, causing a smile to spread across his features. *I love him so much.*

"Hello, dear." Lillian Stanford came to a stop next to Maddie. "You look beautiful." Her smile, so reminiscent of Ring's, radiated warmth and calm.

"Thank you, so do you." Maddie drew in a deep breath. "Are you ready?"

The woman nodded and they exchanged a hug. Maddie turned to Sherri. "It's time."

Sherri turned to the wedding coordinator. "Now."

The blond, her hair knotted in a French twist, spoke into an ear piece. "Cue organ music."

Notes from the pipe organ along with a string section filled the church as guests turned their attention toward the vestibule.

"Cue ring bearer."

"Ring bearer cued," a thin man in Armani replied into his own ear piece as he set Brutus down in the open doorway.

"Come here, Bru." Albie stood at the front of the church, slightly stooped in a tux as he encouraged the dog.

The Pomeranian made his way down the aisle. A small pillow, strapped around his middle, held two simple gold bands. Several "Awws," could be heard as he reached Albie, and the man picked him up. "Good boy, Bru." Albie gave him a hug before placing him in Dave's hands.

"Don't bite me this time, okay?" Dave whispered to the dog as he held him in a awkward grip.

"Cue bridesmaid."

Sherri stepped forward and started down the aisle.

"Bridesmaid cued."

Maddie looked from the wedding planner to her assistant and shook her head. *Really?* They were only about twelve feet apart, but continued to speak in to their ear pieces, their backs to each other.

"Cue maid of honor."

Maddie turned to Lillian. "I'm so happy this is happening."

"Me too." Tears sparkled in the older woman's eyes. "I love you. Thank you for giving my son his life back."

"I said cue maid of honor. Where's the maid of honor?" The question came across as a hiss.

"Thank you both for giving me a second chance at family," Maddie whispered as she reached up and pulled down Lillian's chin length veil before stepping to the doorway.

"Maid of honor cued," the assistant said with a sigh of relief.

"Cue escort. Where's the escort?"

Maddie came to stand by Sherri and turned in time to see the assistant waving from the back. She glanced across the way. Ring smiled at her. "You need to go back there."

He nodded and hurried to the back of the church. The music changed to the bridal chorus and everyone rose as Lillian Stanford, escorted by her son, made her way down the aisle, her dress a creamy antique satin and lace. They came to a stop in front of the altar.

The minister came forward. "Dearly beloved, we are gathered here today in the presence of these witnesses to join Albert Jefferson Norstock and Lillian Josephine Stanford in matrimony. Who gives this woman to be wed?"

"I do." Ring smiled at his mother as the groom joined them. He placed her hand in Albie's before stepping back to stand beside Dave.

"Wonderful. The bride and groom have written vows. Go ahead, Lillian."

"I promise to cherish you for the rest of our days, in sickness and in health until death do us part." She smiled. "Also, I promise to stop trying to get you to eat kale."

Everyone laughed.

Albie shuffled from foot to foot a moment, adjusted his cummerbund and straightened as much as his aged body would allow. "My devotion to you will continue to grow—right to my last day. But my love for you will go on way beyond that because it knows no bounds."

There wasn't a sound in the church.

He pulled out a white handkerchief, scrubbed at his eyes a moment before tucking it away, and cleared his throat a couple of times. "Also, thanks for the kale thing. And I promise not to cheat at pinochle anymore." Albie smiled.

Lillian nodded, her eyes watery and smiled in return.

"The rings?"

Dave stepped forward holding Brutus away from his body as Lillian and Albie unclipped the rings from the pillow.

Albie slid the ring on Lillian's finger. "Lillian, I give you this ring as an eternal symbol of my love and commitment to you."

"Albert, I give you this ring as an eternal symbol of my love and commitment to you."

"By the power vested in me by the State of Vermont, I pronounce you husband and wife. You may now kiss the bride."

Their kiss was brief, but sweet.

"Ladies and gentleman, I present to you Mr. and Mrs. Albert Norstock."

Loud applause filled the church as the recessional music started and the couple worked their way down the aisle.

"What a great turnout." Madison glanced around the room. Lillian and Albie had left for home, as well as a few other elders, but despite the hour, the gymnasium was still packed with people. "It's a great party."

Ring smiled. "I think so too. How about a dance?" He pulled her into his arms and moved out onto the floor. "Do you wish we'd had a big wedding now?"

His words vibrated near Maddie's ear where her head rested on his chest. She pulled back to look up into his face. "No, not all. Our wedding was perfect. Antigua's paradise. And how you managed to keep it out of the papers and still fly most of Northam down there to attend, I'll never know."

He shrugged with a smile. "And I'd do it all again tomorrow if it made you happy."

"I am happy, Ring. I've never been happier." She reached up on tiptoe to meet his lips.

Moments later, a squeal was followed by, "Yes, yes, yes!" Sherri and Dave stood by a hay bale seat. Or at least Dave stood. Sherri was jumping up and down.

Ring laughed. "I take it he asked her."

"That's great." Madison smiled

"Do you think they'll be happy?"

"I do. She's crazy about him. Not to mention, she loves the travel and excitement of different places." Maddie paused. "Don't you miss it sometimes?"

"Nope. Whenever I go, I can't wait to get home. I love my life." Ring gave Madison a tender kiss. "I love my wife." He kissed her again.

"I love you too." She smiled. "And I thank whatever stars aligned to put you in my path—every day."

"Me too." He pulled her closer as they continued to move around the floor. "So, I haven't had time to ask you—any new disasters on the Harvest Ball front I should know about before someone approaches me?"

"Are you serious?"

He nodded. "Of course. I take my job as honorary chairman seriously."

She gave a delicate snort. "You're honorary chairman because they like your money."

He shrugged. "It's a start."

"Well, let's see." Madison looked the crowd over. "See that blonde over there? That's Blair Whitman—you haven't met her yet. We have to make sure she doesn't stuff the ballot box this year. What else? Oh yeah, word is Marv Carter's switched from hard cider to moonshine, so we'll have to keep an eye on him." Madison smiled. "Oh, and here's a good one. Willa Mae just came up with this one about an hour ago—after several trips to the open bar. She thinks we should do some impromptu fund raising tonight for the Bandstand Beautification project. Get this...she's suggesting you should man a kissing booth and gave me this to start you off. She wants to be first in line." Madison held up a one-dollar bill. "I said I'd check with you—not!"

"It's good to be home." Ring laughed as he whirled his wife around the floor. "I love my life."

# Author's Note

Reviews spread the word of an enjoyed book and are the best way to thank an author for their hard work. Please leave a short review on your favorite book site.

# About the Author

C. L. Howland loves creating stories of everyday people caught up in the sometimes extraordinary business of living. When not plotting what challenges her characters will face next, C. L. enjoys life with her family in the Green Mountains of Vermont.

To learn more about C. L., or to sign up
for her mailing list, please visit:
**www.clhowland.com**

# My Mother Grows *Wallflowers*

There isn't a heck of a lot that doesn't scream target about Mina Mason: her weight, her homemade dresses, even the hoarder's paradise loosely disguised as the Masons' home. Samuel Two Bears Miller reshapes Mina's understated existence with his arrival, his dark skin and long braid exotic next to the Puritan pallor of the local boys. All through high school, Mina conceals her odd home life behind the closed doors of her dilapidated house, even after discovering love with the outspoken boy. Mina must choose between the person who makes her feel alive and the family who relies on her.

**Now Available at Major Online Retailers**

Legacy of a *Wallflower*

C.L. Howland

Flashing blue lights and a pink sandal in the middle of a rural Vermont road mark the end of a dream for Mina Mason as a tragic accident halts her elopement to Sam Miller. No one's ever been allowed inside the Mason's shabby house. That rule isn't about to change, leaving Mina to care for her aging mother amid piles of hoarded possessions. With no respite in sight, Mina breaks her engagement to Sam. He deserves the normal life he'll never find with her.

**Now Available at Major Online Retailers**

Forced from her home by the tragedy of Pearl Harbor, Elizabeth Wellman hides in plain sight in the city of Bayonne, New Jersey. But she can't escape her memories, and long sleeves can't conceal all her scars.

Dante Montenari, an injured war hero, ignores his own loneliness—until Elizabeth Wellman finds her way into his life and his heart.

When these two solitary souls become entangled in a territorial clash between the Irish and Italian mobs, will fate step in and give them another chance...at life and at love?

**Now Available at Major Online Retailers**